Choosing To Love A Lady Thug 3

TN Jones

Choosing To Love A Lady Thug 3 © 2017 by TN Jones

Cover designed by Bryant Sparks

This book is a work of fiction. Names, characters, places, and incidents either are products of the author's imagination or are used fictitiously. Any resemblance to actual persons, living or dead, events, or locales is entirely coincidental.

Acknowledgment

First, thanks must go out to the Higher Being for providing me with a sound body and mind; in addition to having the natural talent of writing and blessing me with the ability to tap into such an amazing part of life. Second, thanks most definitely go out to my Princess. Third, to my supporters and new readers for giving me a chance. Where in the world would I be without y'all?

Truth be told, I wouldn't have made it this far without anyone. I truly thank everyone for rocking with me. MUAH! Y'all make this writing journey enjoyable! I would like to thank everyone from the bottom of my heart for always rocking with the novelist kid from Alabama, no matter what I drop. Y'all have once again trusted me to provide y'all with quality entertainment.

Enjoy, my loves!

Chapter One

Flema

Friday, December 8, 2017

When I finally came too, the sun was shining brightly and I was lying in my bed with Wilema, softly stroking my hair as she said softly, "I'm glad you are awake. I was afraid that Fish really hurt you last night."

Looking at her strangely, I pushed her body away from me as I stood up in the bed. The last thing I remembered before Fish knocked me to the floor was him telling me about Juvy and Wilema. Trying to remember everything that happened, I sort of struggled with the memory. After some time, things started to come back clearly. I clearly remembered Bone throwing Wilema over his shoulder and walking her out of my home. With a frown on my face, I wondered what made him change his mind, and I surely asked her.

"Why did Bone let you stay?" I said lightly as I placed my back against the headboard.

"Because Fish told him to do so, that I would be useless and so are you," she replied, placing her hands on top of mine and massaging them.

Quickly snatching my hands back and analyzing my sister's eyes, I had to inquire on the subject that Fish said to me last night.

"Have you ever fucked Juvy, Wilema?"

"Hell fuck no, Flema. Why in the hell would you ask me that question?" she asked curiously.

Before I responded, I studied her body language. I had a way of knowing if my sister was lying or not, and as I surveilled her body and eyes I knew she wasn't lying to me.

"Before I passed out last night, Fish said that you had gotten pregnant by Juvy twice and gave the children away," I said softly as I kept my eyes on Wilema.

With a smirk on her face, she snickered lightly before saying, "Look how you called that nigga out, Flema. I would say anything to piss you off."

Thinking back to what I said about two of Fish's children not being his, but Juvy's instead, I saw what gave him ammunition to say those hurtful things to me. As I laughed off the foolishness that Fish said, my sister and I started talking about what Juvy could've done to piss Bone and Fish off. While Wilema cooked breakfast, the real talk came about; one that I wished could've waited since I didn't want to talk about my period being late.

"What are you going to do if you are?" she asked flipping over the bacon.

"Stop the foolishness and become a mom."

"Are you going to reach out to Juvy?"

"No. He's in enough shit as it is. Plus, the less he knows the better. I'm serious about not having him in my life anymore, Wilema. I've done too much shit for him to be treated any other way than a queen," I said as my voice broke by the end of my response.

"You live and you learn, love. Let this be a lesson for you, okay?" Wilema said as she took the bacon out of the skillet, turned off the grits, and pulled the biscuits out of the oven.

As she gave me a life lesson on men and love, I took in everything that she said. I wished I had listened to her years ago when I really became heavily involved with Juvy. As I cried until I couldn't anymore, breakfast was served. Taking a hot relaxing shower, Wilema busted in the bathroom and told me to get dressed. Anxious to know where she was taking me, I quickly bathed and hopped out of the shower.

A half hour later, Wilema had me in every store on the east side of Miami. Store after store, I was about to lose my damn mind. My legs were tired and I grew tired of saying excuse me. It was the busiest and most important time of the year, close to Christmas, and people were out shopping and enjoying family that flew in. At 3:30 p.m., I had to tell Wilema that I had enough of shopping and being around people.

"Okay. Can we go and get our nails and toes done... my treat?" she whined in a child-like voice.

Knowing that getting a pedicure and getting my nails done was a sure way to keep me out and about, I agreed with a wide grin on my face.

"Sweet!" she yelled soon as we walked out of Dillard's, heading toward her car.

On the way toward our favorite nail shop, Luv Nail Shop, I thought about how my life would change if I was indeed pregnant. I would have to get a job and be more responsible. I would have to get me a car and stop relying on Juvy to take me places. My life could possibly do a three-sixty if my period didn't come on. Anxiety was growing in me rapidly, and I had to know what was up. Coming close to a CVS, I asked Wilema to pull into the parking lot.

"Do you want anything to drink or a snack out of here?" I asked as I secured my purse on my right shoulder and opened the door to her car.

"Trail mix and a water, please."

"Sure thing. I love you, Wilema, and thank you for getting me out of the house today."

"You are welcome. Haven't I always been there for you?"

"Yes."

"And trust... it's never going to stop."

With a thankful smile on my face, I jumped out of her car, aiming for the entrance door. Upon walking into the chilly establishment, I spoke to the cashier and the beautiful couple that was standing at the counter. Sashaying toward the pregnancy tests, my heart was heavily beating, and the palms of my hands were sweaty. Snatching up the two pregnancy tests in the EPT box, I quickly walked back to the front of CVS. Before I made it to the register, I grabbed a bag of trail mix and a bottled water.

Mind on a million, I placed the items on the counter and pulled out a twenty-dollar bill. After the cashier rang up my items, I politely thanked him and went on about my business. Once in the car, I handed my sister her items and tucked mine inside of my purse. K-Camp's song "2Crazy" played on the radio, causing Wilema to turn the volume up. While the song was playing, my mind took me down memory lane.

When the song first came out, I gave Juvy a wonderful show that had us held hostage in my house for an entire day and night. The loving he rendered me was mind blowing; I don't know what was wrong with him that particular night, but he left nothing on my body untouched by his hands, mouth, and dick. It was my first time trying anal, and needless to say, I fucking loved it! Ever since then, I tried to have it incorporated into our sex lives; well except when he was pissed off. That nigga had too much dick to be receiving in the ass.

"Helllloooo," Wilema shouted in my face as her right hand was shaking me.

"Yeah," I replied, snapping out of the zone.

"Come on in here so that we can finish our girl time while Kym and Zym handle our business, sis," she said before closing the driver's door.

Getting out of the car, I shook my head and sighed lazily as I had to get ready for the latest gossip from Kym and Zym; they are twin sisters and knew everybody's business—hell including mine. Wilema and I have been going to the ghetto divas since they were doing nails and toes in their parents' backyard. Those hoes were hella good when it came down to designing and polishing acrylic nails.

Peeking in the door to see how many people were in front of Wilema and me, I was relieved that we were the only two. Soon as I stepped foot in their establishment the foolishness began, "Look at this bougie bitch here!"

"Whatever, Kym," I laughed as I strolled to the bathroom so that I could piss on those sticks.

"Don't be fucking up our bathroom!" Zym joked in her high-pitched voice as I opened the beige door of the bathroom.

"I'm finna blow it up!" I yelled as I closed the door behind me.

"Lord, please let this thing be negative. I don't need any more negative things in my life. I know I will be a great mother one day, but right now isn't the best time," I said as I pulled down my pants and panties, followed by sitting down on the freshly cleaned toilet.

Feeling myself about to piss, I quickly unwrapped the pregnancy test box and pulled one out. Once I opened the protective paper, I threw it on the floor, pulled off the top, and unleashed all of my piss on the stick. I know that was unnecessary but I wanted the test to have all of my urine.

After I placed the test on the floor, I wiped my ass and proceeded to pull up my clothing. My nerves got the best of me, so I decided to whistle one of Wilema's tunes that always brought me back to the level that I needed to be on—calm. Intuition told me to turn around, snatch the test up and look at it; therefore, I did just that.

"Fuck! Fuck!" I stated in a low tone.

I couldn't believe that I was looking at two strong pink lines. Most women would be excited to know that they were pregnant, but I wasn't. I was pissed because of who the father was, how I handled myself for him, and knowing that he wasn't a father to the kids that Tania had. Without a doubt, he wasn't going to do shit for mine.

Feeling like complete shit, I was ready to go home and cry my damn eyes out. Once my mother gets a whiff of this news, she was going to be down my damn throat. While I strolled toward the pedicure chair that Zym told me to sit at, Wilema asked, "What's wrong?"

Biting down on my lip and avoiding eye contact with all of them, I simply replied, "I'm pregnant."

"Ohh, bitch. What are you going to do?" Kym asked as she put the moisturizing petals into Wilema's pedicure water.

"Be a mom... a responsible mom," I replied as I looked into my sister's disturbed face.

"I will have your back every step of the way," my sister announced in a disappointed tone.

"Thank you because I will need you."

I was thankful that the twins didn't attempt to touch my delicate situation. All I could think about was the life I was going to bring into the world, and how I had to be a strong, positive example for my child.

Enjoying the hot water on my feet, I pulled out my phone and texted Juvy a photo of the pregnancy test.

Me: *I'm not doing this to get you back. If you want to be a father to our child, you are more than welcome to do so. I'm not going to be one of those bitter women. We can be cordial with one another as we raise our child.*

Me: *You need to stay away from Bone and Fish... those niggas ain't right at all.*

The entire time that I was texting Juvy, I noticed that Wilema was looking at me. Quickly closing out my text message, I pulled my headphones out of my purse, stuck them in the headphone jack, and selected a nice, soothing playlist. As the soft beat and strong, powerful voice of Dorothy Moore blasted through the speakers, I closed my eyes and relived the moments of my childhood, prior to Juvy. I was one happy child; always hopping, skipping, and smiling. I never had to worry about anything, because my mother made sure that I nor my sister wanted for anything. Now, I prayed that she would be there for me as I traveled down a new journey as an expectant mother.

You are going to be okay, Flema. You and this child will be fine. Your mother will be mad at you, but not for long. Wilema and your mother will make sure that you are okay, I thought as the song "Misty Blue" continued to play in my ear.

Chapter Two

Tony

I was awakened by the strong numbing sensation that was running through my shoulder blades, arms, and fingers. The pain was unreal; I couldn't tolerate it anymore, thus me going down memory lane so that I could take my mind off it; plus, going down that lane would help me finesse my way out of the situation I was in with X. One of the memory lanes that came to the forefront of my mind was when Sabrina was constantly saying smart shit to X, which began in the later months of 2012.

"What the hell is going on with your phone?" I asked X while I wrapped my arms around her waist. That damn phone been vibrating for the past two hours.

"Someone been calling me from a private number and I'm placing the calls on the reject list. Is it possible that little bitch, Sabrina, got my number?"

"Nope. My phone stay locked."

"Okay," she replied curtly.

"Look, can't no one get your number from me. It can't be her because she doesn't know my unlock code to get it," I said seriously as I turned her around to face me. She nodded her head and kissed me on the forehead.

"Was I really just a nut to you?" she asked with a sad look in her eyes.

"Hell no, don't pay that girl no mind. She's just mad."

"Tony, don't fuck with me. Be honest with me at all times,"

"I will forever be honest with you, X'Zeryka."

That particular day I was dead serious about forever being honest with her. I hoped that she believed everything I said because I was done with the games. X completed me for real. I never had a person that helped me the way she had. No matter how much or how badly I hurt her feelings, she was right there to pick a nigga up and let me know that everything would be alright.

Over the course of the years we had been messing around, I never had a female that talked more positivity in me than she did— especially when it came down to my children. X had an entirely different approach when she tried to make me see things in a different way. She didn't nag or criticize me; a young guy like me was used to that from Marsha, my momma, and the idiots that I had children with. No matter if the decision was easy or hard, I went to X with the problem, and she made me sit down and write the pros and cons of the issue, thus bringing myself to a solution.

If I had been true to my word, I wouldn't have been in the situation that I was in. If I would've kept things one thousand with her, I wouldn't be outstretched in a damn barn with my shoulders feeling like they were about to break off. I knew what I was up against if things turned out for the worst between X and me; a part of me felt like she loved me so that it wouldn't have come down to this, but I was dead as wrong.

I knew she deeply cared about a nigga when we had this particular conversation.

"Remember back when my car fucked up, and I was walking to and from work in the cold?" I asked, looking down at X.

"Yeah, why?"

"I'm just reminiscing, that's all."

"Why?"

"Sometimes I do that when I'm trying to figure things out."

"Seeing how much of a dummy I am for you," she replied as she stared into my eyes.

"You were not, and still aren't, dumb for me. Don't you ever say that."

"I was dumb for you back then, and somewhat still am. Oh yeah, I found out why you didn't let me pick you up or drop you off when didn't have a car," she stated, fumbling with her fingers. I looked at her quizzically because I knew damn well she didn't know why; if she did, she would've been threw it up in my face.

"This is my last time saying that you are not dumb for me, and I bet you don't know why I wouldn't let you pick me up or drop me off from work," I joked.

"You were staying with JaJa and her folks. Marsha had put you out," she spat in a nonchalant, matter-of-fact voice. The look on my face was

priceless. I wanted to know how in the hell did she know that shit, so of course I asked.

"How did you know that?"

"I'm the Queen. I have eyes and ears everywhere. I also have several different cars that you or my family don't even know about. Plus, I make sure that you are okay when we aren't talking... so I have Baked and J-Money keep an eye out on you from time to time. The only thing they reported back to me was that you were okay. I made sure to tell them don't tell me shit about your relationship. Shit, I got off topic just that quick... mmm, yeah, I found out about you and JaJa when I was in one of my secret cars and saw you grabbing the chick hand as y'all walked into a bricked, red house on the North side of Montgomery. When I described the broad to the J-Money and Baked, they watched out for you, and informed me that ole girl was your girl."

As I strolled down that memory lane, I noticed how X didn't keep eye contact or hold on to my hand; that let me know that she was really struggling with me being committed to other females—especially after I told her that I loved her, and I showed it. Feeling bad about how things were playing out between the two of us had me feeling sour. I couldn't take anything back that I did to her, but I could make her see that I was truly sorry for hurting and betraying her. The only thing that held me back from genuinely showing it to her was the fact that she didn't allow me to speak when she walked inside of the barn.

The only person I could turn to was God; therefore, I closed my eyes and began to pray.

Dear God, It's me, Tony, again. I want out of this situation I have placed myself in. There is a lesson to be learned, and I have my eyes opened so that I could receive the message. I know my wrongs in messing over women's hearts, and I won't do it again. I've asked for your forgiveness in my wrongdoings. Now, I need X's forgiveness. Will you help me in showing her that I am truly sorry for betraying and hurting her? After this incident is over with, I will be a humble servant for you, Lord.

Feeling great about the prayer that I sent out, I felt good about my situation even though I didn't know what to expect when X returned.

X

The sun's rays greeted me before I had the chance to throw the red cover over my head. Feeling a stern pop to my ass let me knew that I was not in the bed alone. Rolling over to see a smiling Rondon caused me to sigh heavily and turn back over. Thinking about the strategy that my goons and I planned for Francesco and Reggio would go wonderfully, and I was ready to implement the plan. All I had to do was keep my body under wraps, which shouldn't be any problems. Any little fuck up from me would threaten my future plans—being criminally free.

"Oh, so you ain't excited to see your baby daddy?" he joked in a low tone.

"Why in the hell are you in here, again? Where are the others?" I asked from underneath the covers.

"Probably sleep," he replied as he snatched the cover off my body and roughly placed me on my back.

Looking at him as he climbed on top of me, I was hoping that he wasn't going to try anything stupid or I would have to explain some shit that I wasn't ready for. Spreading my legs and climbing in between them, Rondon kissed my inner thighs all the while lightly thumbing my rising bud.

"Hmmm," I moaned lowly as the thought approached for me to push him away from me.

Going to complete what my thought suggested, it was too late because that fool inserted his magical fingers and I began to ride them. Feeling an orgasm approaching, I quickly covered my mouth and let it escape into my hands. Laughing while pleasuring me, Rondon decided that he wanted to go above and beyond to let *us* be known.

"I see your nasty ass is loving that, huh?" he said loud enough for my crew to hear the conversation if they were awake.

"You are too loud... now be quiet," I stated sternly through clenched teeth.

"I told you once and I'll tell you again... in the streets you are the boss but in the bedroom, I own that ass! This is when I show you who the boss is," he said as he slid his face toward mine and planted his lips on top of mine. Strongly pushing my legs up behind my head, I felt uncomfortable and my face showed it.

"What's wrong with you?" Rondon asked as he lifted his head up to look at me.

"Nothing," I lied while bringing my legs down to his waist.

"I want those legs behind your head, X," he announced, placing them back where he had them.

Wanting to tell him that it was uncomfortable to be in that position, I decided against it since he knew how to make me bow down when we were in the bedroom. With my legs tucked behind my head, my lower abdomen region was stretching and pulling all sorts of ways. Rondon kissed my lips gently while caressing my titties, which felt damn good. Leaving a trail of kisses from my lips to my breasts, Rondon stuck his man inside of me, which caused me to gasp loudly.

Laughing, he continued to toy and stroke my extremely hot and wet pussy; truth be told I didn't know I was in the mood for that type of action. Slowly stroking my girl, Rondon stared into my face as he passionately devoured my girl. Orgasm after orgasm consumed me within minutes and his tongue was in my mouth as I moaned, masking my beautiful cries.

Somewhere around the thirtieth stroke, that damn switch flipped in his head and he went insane and there wasn't a damn thing that I could do about it. The bed went bananas as he rocked my body all sorts of ways; wanting to tell him to get up, I couldn't because my pussy had one mean hold on those inches of chocolaty dick.

With his mouth to my ear, Rondon spat, "You think it was cool to fuck that nigga, Juvy?"

Shocked at the question, I closed my eyes and prayed that he would tone down.

"I asked you a fucking question... now answer me," he piped as he dug deeper inside of me which caused me to call out his name.

"Okay, Ms. 'I don't have to answer to anybody but me'."

Why in the hell couldn't I just answer the damn question? Because I was one arrogant asshole, that truly felt that she didn't have to answer to anyone. That nigga put a blessing on my pussy and the only thing I could say was, "Rondon, you are hurting me."

"Hurting you? Nawl, that's impossible. You are fucking Queenpin. Your kind don't have feelings," he spat before pulling himself out of me and roughly rolling me onto my stomach before slamming his manhood inside of me which caused my head to hit the headboard.

"Ouch," I mumbled before dipping my head into the firm pillow.

Rondon was pounding my pussy out when I heard Baked yelling before laughing, "I knew Chief was pregnant."

Fuck! I thought I buried that shit in the bottom of the trash can. What in the fuck was he doing to find it anyways, I thought at the same time Rondon pulled out of me and said sternly to my back, "Who's responsible for getting you pregnant, X?"

Lifting my head away from the pillow and halfway turning my head toward my most handsome killer, I replied while biting down on my lip, "You."

"That's what I don't believe. I want a DNA test," he confessed as he got out of bed and put on his clothes.

Feeling like complete shit, I angrily stared at him because deep down I knew he was going to hit me with that shit. Before I knew it, I lashed out on his ass. Jumping out of the bed, I ran toward him with balled fists and pummeled his face. While I was attacking his face, Rondon picked me up and dunked me on the bed.

With my wrists tightly bound in his hand, I spat before tearing up, "I hate you. You ain't no better than the next. Now, I see why Tyke said fuck love! I knew you were going to do me like this. I want you the fuck off my crew immediately!"

"Who have you fucked without a rubber besides me, X?" Rondon yelled loudly.

"I said no motherfucking body but you! You don't have to worry about me or my kid... we gonna be motherfuckin' good! You forgot who in the fuck puts money in your hands monthly, nigga! Now, get the fuck out of my face. As of now, I'm not X to you! I'm just that bitch to you!" I said angrily at the same time I heard J-Money, Baked, and Ruger say, "Ahh shit."

"Ruger!!" I yelled as the tears flowed down my cheeks while Rondon glared at me.

"Yes, Chief," he called from the door.

"Get this motherfucker away from me and make sure that he stays away from me!" I screamed, trying not to cry.

"Ruger, don't come in here... she doesn't have on any clothes," Rondon announced as he wiped my tears away.

"I'm sorry I said that to you. I know the baby is mine. I know what type of female you are. I know you are very protective of that pussy," Rondon said to me as he released my hands and slid down my body to kiss my abdomen.

Quickly resuming to 'that' X, I pushed him up off me and glared down at him. Sinisterly laughing, I shoved him on the floor, causing his head to hit the floor. I knew I had the look of death mixed in with hurt in my eyes because he kept saying that he was sorry and that he was honored to be a father.

Fighting between my evil and calm side, I chose to let my calm side talk and respond to him, "Stay the fuck away from me. It's over between us. You said the one thing that killed us for life."

Getting up off him, I unlocked my bedroom door and threw on some clothes. On the way out of my room, I didn't care that my goons were looking at me, I didn't care that Rondon was calling my name, and I simply didn't care that my goons knew that I was pregnant by Rondon!

Upon the slamming of the condo's door, the tears seeped down my face and I felt like a complete lost soul. Halfway down the hallway, I heard Ruger shouting out my name.

"I can't talk right now, Ruger. I have too much shit on my plate. I don't need you to tell me that I fucked up! I know this okay!" I shouted, not turning around to properly address him.

"I'm not going to chastise you, X. I just want to make sure that you are okay. Things are changing for you and I'm not the only one that notices it. I been knew about you and Rondon," he blurted out, which caused me to stop walking.

Turning around, I said, "How?"

Chuckling, Ruger replied in his deep voice, "Hmm... you forget that Rondon and I are number one and number two. You forget that we tell each other everything. I been knew how he felt for you. I've made myself unavailable so that Rondon could be around you more; so that he could have some of my tasks of reading to you or dealing with you when you are on your period. I was the reason why he knows so much about you."

"Explain, now," I said, strolling toward the man that had my back since I was sixteen years old.

"He needs to explain... not me."

"We were supposed to be keeping an eye on all of them," I said in a matter-of-fact tone.

"True, but after he told me something that I didn't know and I verified it... I knew he was harmless and that his intentions toward you were indeed great."

Not caring what information that Rondon brought to Ruger, I replied blankly before turning around to walk away, "I'm going to the beach to think. I can't think with y'all in my face."

"Tyke... I did that... not Barry," Rondon yelled as I pressed the down button on the elevator's silver panel.

"Give her some time, Rondon... give her some time. She didn't ask me what information you brought to me, so I know she's processing things differently right now," I heard Ruger say as the elevator dinged and I quickly hopped on it.

***

While I was on the beach I had time to think about my life and the life I was carrying. I wanted a change, and the only way to do that was through accepting that I was going to be a mother and a damn good one. There would be no abortion or miscarriage this time; this pregnancy was going to be the reason I escaped the game for good! I knew that I had to leave my past behind and provide a better one for the little life that didn't have a heartbeat. I had to change from the evil person that I was to a loving person. I couldn't change overnight, but I knew that with time and patience I would be the woman that my grandmother meant for me to be.

While I was on that beach crying and thinking, I came up with the perfect idea to get me the hell out of Miami with my tasks completed. Running like hell away from the beach back to my condo, not talking to any of my goons until I made the date with Francesco; that was when I informed them of the play. Everyone agreed and I took my ass to sleep, with Rondon behind me and his left hand on my stomach.

Four hours later, I had to push my personal issues to the side as I slipped on a beautiful white strapless dress and a pair of white heels. Pearls were around my neck and wrists as I had one pearl-studded gold ring on my right ring finger and a pair of studded pearl earrings. The first couple of rows of my box braids were twisted and the remaining braids were pulled into a high ponytail. Never being the type to wear makeup, tonight I did because it was going to be a special event between Francesco and me.

"You look beautiful, X," Rondon said as he kissed the nape of my neck.

"Thanks," I replied dryly.

"We need to talk soon as we are on the airplane."

"You said what you had to say, and I said what I had to say. We good," I replied before walking out of my room and snatching the keys off the counter.

"X!" Rondon yelled.

"You don't get to call me fucking X. It's Chief to you!" I screamed angrily while turning on my heels to reinforce his position.

Meanwhile, J-Money, Baked, and Ruger sat on the black, trimmed in gold couch glancing in between Rondon and me. While I was ignoring their stares, Rondon reinforced them to say something.

They shrugged their shoulders as J-Money replied to Rondon, "You shouldn't have said whatever you said, bruh. You know she takes words to the heart, so only you can fix what you have done. We ain't got nothing to do with this. I told yo' ass Chief ain't ordinary... she eats while shitting, and she can have a full-blown conversation with Ruger while he's on the shitbox! She eats damn sushi, sardines, oysters, and chitlins'..."

Wanting to be angry, I couldn't because J-Money's remark had me tickled; therefore, I stated in a fake defensive timbre, "That is so not true."

"Lies, Chief, lies," they all responded while laughing, minus Rondon.

At that moment, I realized that my goons were more than just my goons; they were my family. They were the only ones that knew me so well. If I had a question I didn't go to a random person, I went to them. It was clear that I knew everything about them, and they knew everything about me.

"I want to be a father to my child, X," Rondon announced sternly, clearly defying what I told him about calling me X.

Ignoring him, I said, "Fellas let's get this shit on the road. Time to finish this one task and move on to another."

"Chief, after all of this is done... we gotta properly pay our respects to Silky Snake's family. His mom is still taking his death hard," Baked interjected.

Looking at him, I replied, "We most definitely have to do that. Have any of DB's family tried reaching out to anyone of you?"

"No. He's used to not talking to them for a month at a time," J-Money responded, rubbing his hands together.

"Cool. Silky Snake was the only one that met his family, right?" I inquired, making sure that I didn't have to come up with a fake missing report mission.

"Correct, Chief," they all responded.

Nodding my head, I signaled that particular conversation was over with.

Knock. Knock. Knock.

As I looked at the door, Rondon's ugly ass was walking toward it. When he opened it, I gasped loudly. Standing handsomely in an all-black tuxedo with a red handkerchief inside of the breast pocket, Juvy spoke dryly to Rondon before walking in. Rondon had a look on his face that let me knew he was ready to tear up my condo, but I made sure that he saw that I wasn't in the mood before the condo's door closed.

"How y'all doing?" Juvy spoke to everyone.

"Good. What 'bout you?" J-Money asked him as Baked and Ruger analyzed him.

"As good as I'm gonna get," he informed them before looking at me.

"You good, Ma?"

"My response is the same as yours, Juvian," I told him as I held his gaze.

"Ma, it would be important to at least turn your phone on," he replied in that sexy sultry voice of his.

"You don't need to worry about her damn phone dude. She ain't your woman," Rondon spat after he slammed his fist down on the counter.

"She ain't yours either... now is she, *dude*," Juvy shouted as he turned around to stare Rondon down.

"What in the fuck have I missed?" Baked asked quizzically at the same time J-Money said, "Shit, I'm saying. Catch a nigga up to speed, Ruger."

Not up for the shit that Rondon and Juvy were about to set off, I let my voice ring loud and clear.

"One thing y'all fuckers ain't finna do is fucking irritate my soul. It's already doing numbers, so can y'all please stay on the tasks at hand, Rondon and Juvy," I spat to those ignorant asses that I fucked.

Nodding their heads, all eyes fell back on me, and Juvy spoke.

"Before I was rudely interrupted, Ma, I was trying to reach out to you last night because I remembered a conversation that took place while I was at the gas station when I first touched down. It was from a chick named... named...shit, it's on the tip of my tongue," Juvy stated as he looked up to the ceiling before saying, "Taea. This chick was talking to a nigga named Bango about sealing the deal on you and that she was tired of waiting."

After Juvy was done talking, my goons were in full throttle surrounding me and Juvy. They were asking for full details about when and where he saw Bango and Taea. As Juvy told us about the conversation between Bango and Taea, I was ready to faint. Trying my best to get a handle on my heartbeat and thoughts, I began to think about the kills that I had to complete. That was the only way I knew how to hold things together; since I still had several more missions to complete before I officially dealt with Bango. Overindulging on the thoughts of Bango would cause my life to end!

"We have to get to moving. Francesco is waiting on me. Y'all leave and get in those positions. Remember, soon as I give the signal... drop his bodyguards. Juvy and I will take care of Francesco. Also, Ruger, I need your girls to tell me what Reggio is doing as we speak," I announced with an anxious voice. After the shootout yesterday, Reggio and his brother fled the scene to one of Ruger's whore houses.

"Yes, Chief," they all replied minus Rondon and Juvy.

As Ruger walked onto the balcony to make the call, I was grateful that the fellas decided to strategize on a way to drag Bango, Taea, Reggio, and Dundo to the front of the crowd. While they talked, I thought about the one person that introduced loving a man in the first place... Marcus 'Bango' Johnson. I felt the tears sliding down my face as I thought about our history.

Six minutes later, Ruger was informing me on the whereabouts of the miscreants. With a huge grin on my face, I was ecstatic that they were falling for my lovely bait. The plan I had for those fuckers was like a delicate, beautifully decorated wedding cake; it was just that fucking sweet and gorgeous!

Before we exited the condo, Rondon made it his business to drop to his knees, kiss my stomach, and mouthed something. I assumed that he said a prayer, and I was right on that assumption.

J-Money asked him what did he say, and his response was, "I said a safe return prayer for my child and my woman, and told my unborn seed that I love him or her."

Placing his eyes on me, Rondon continued, "I love you just as much as I love the embryo you are carrying, X."

With the smack of my lips and a smirk on my face, I left Rondon right where his ass was at. I wasn't in the mood for the sentimental shit. I was on a kill mission, and I needed everyone on the same boat as me. I couldn't mix my feelings with business; that was a for sure way to get killed. However, I had some shit to deal with once I got back on that damn airplane ranging from my past to my baby daddy!

Chapter Four

Juvy

It was 5:45 p.m. when I strolled through the back door of Chivalry; thanks to one of Ruger's trusted gal pals that worked in the restaurant. One thing I knew for certain was that X and her boys had some strong ass connections; they knew damn near the entire world. They truly had pull. I was anxious to get the show on the road so that I could have my answers, see Francesco die, and finally have a grown-up conversation with Flema about the pregnancy.

Chivalry was an upscale eating establishment. They served everything minus soul food. Delicious, exquisite main course dishes and a gorgeous presentation for dessert had them in the top twenty places to eat in Miami. Top-notch wine and liquor that was deemed vintage. Upon entry of the beautifully decorated gold and ivory restaurant, candles were everywhere. Two candles were lit on each table and surrounding brown banisters. Soft melodies played through the eating establishment. The vibe of the place was intended to make visitors feel welcomed and relaxed. There were two eating areas; both large and decorated the same way. Gorgeous oversized portraits hung on the walls of the eating area surely had my eyes logged in, whenever I frequented the place.

Throughout the entire time I was in the kitchen area of Chivalry, Flema's text message kept replaying in my head. The last thing I needed was for her to be with child. Her being pregnant would cause some severe issues that I wasn't up for. All that nagging, constantly calling and texting, and wondering why I haven't been by the previous day were a recipe for arguments. If Flema was going to be true to her word about strictly co-parenting than I would be fine with that, but I had to come clean about some shit, first.

Exhaling deeply, I knew I had to put my personal feelings to the side for this mission, because, like X stated, it could get me killed.

"Can you hear me?" Ruger's deep voice boomed through the small, clear earpiece in my right ear, interrupting my thoughts.

"Yeah," I replied as I quickly grabbed the white chef jacket and hat off the tall stainless steel rack that was close to the entrance door of the kitchen.

As I was fixing the chef coat, the top chef waltzed her short self inside and started barking orders. While she spat out everyone's tasks, she sternly but quickly looked at us. Placing her eyes on me, I stood strongly and eyed her back.

"Who in the hell are you?" her manly voice questioned as her bulging eyes looked me up and down.

"James Tockton," I stated proudly, which was the fake name that Ruger announced in my ear, followed by him telling me to hand her the papers that were safely tucked inside of my tuxedo pocket.

After I handed her my credentials, she shoved them back into my hands and told me, "We have enough chefs but I do need you to help the waitresses to deliver food."

"That's fine with me, ma'am," I informed her with my pearly golds hidden behind my bottom lip.

With ten minutes until our show was to start, I made myself useful to the actual workers of Chivalry, until Ruger said that it was time for the play to begin. I had no idea how things would turn out until the very end. My task was to put some mixed concoction into Francesco's food. Once X gave the signal, then I would take a seat at Francesco's and X's table, thus getting my answers. My hands were antsy to be wrapped around his neck. I couldn't wait to see him die or know that he was close to dying before I disappeared the same way I came—the back door.

Thirty minutes of parading around the huge kitchen with the real cooks, and I learned a lot about the correct temperature of food, how to store it properly, and how to get ahead of the rush hour. One female, in general, showed her behind when it came down to chopping and cutting her vegetables. I was in awe of how she precisely and quickly cut the food small without cutting her fingers.

As I was about to say something to the woman, Ruger's voice boomed through the earpiece, "X and Francesco are walking in the building. His boys stayed in the car, per Francesco's request."

I coughed lightly, signaling him that I heard him. He and X gave me a series of codes to use when I was around people; coughing, sniffling, and sneezing were the codes of acknowledgment.

"It's show time, people, the doors are officially open, and it seems like it's going to be a full house this evening. As usual, no fucking off. Get the orders out, and let's have a good night," the top chef announced sternly and loudly as she stood at the back of the kitchen.

"They are sitting in section six. That's far in the back. It'll be only them. Chie will be sitting in front of him. Meaning Francesco will not see you unless he turns his head," Ruger said lightly.

I sniffled, signaling that I heard what he said.

"Umm. Excuse me, I will need your help with serving some of my tables," the fair-skinned woman with a beautiful shape informed me as she winked her eye twice while smiling. She was the same woman that let me in before all the other kitchen staff arrived.

"Sure thing," I replied, nodding my head.

The woman told me to follow her and I did just that. As she got her workstation ready, we made simple conversation. Within five minutes of us being at her workstation, an order from Francesco and X came through, and I was beyond excited.

"Chicken Caesar salad with almonds with a lightly grilled salmon and an order of a house salad minus onions and extra Italian dressing is on the menu for tonight," the woman told me as she grabbed the plates to decorate them, followed by telling me to place the salmon on the grill.

"Francesco ordered the grilled salmon. Put the concoction in the meat once it's done," Ruger instructed.

Coughing lightly as I turned my head away from the food, the woman waltzed to the mini platinum fridge and gathered items that she needed. Fifteen minutes later, I was helping the waitress deliver the food to X and Francesco. He was so busy staring into X's face that he didn't care to look up and see that I was in his presence. Walking away from the table, I had to admit to myself that X was one beautiful, intelligent woman. She was elegant as she sat at the table wearing a beautiful ivory strapless dress and pearls around her neck and wrists. The jewelry and makeup she wore complimented her well.

Back in the kitchen, I waited patiently for Ruger to tell me to get my ass back to X and Francesco. I went the extra mile and put some of the liquid that I had in a small, clear container in the nigga's salad; I made sure I mouthed to X not to eat any of his food.

The woman and I were talking lightly when I heard Ruger's voice," He's getting woozy and he's running his mouth... get over there."

"On it," I replied as I looked at the woman, who mouthed *good luck.*

Leaving the kitchen, I made a pit stop at the bathroom and trashed the chef coat and hat. Fixing my clothing, I smiled mischievously and waltzed out of the bathroom. With a wide smile on her face, X said, "Francesco, your time has come to answer questions followed by dying."

Turning his head to look at me, that fucker looked at me and smiled before saying, "Juvy." I stood to the side and began my interrogation.

"Why was my family killed?"

"The families weren't supposed to have been killed, just ruffled," his groggy voice stated as his body moved from side to side.

"What prompted you to come to Jundo's Village?" I asked, glaring down at his wobbling body.

"It wasn't my idea, honestly. One of my partners, Reggio Esposito, was behind extorting the people of Jundo's Village for y'all gems and diamonds."

At the sound of Reggio Esposito, X gasped followed by growling. I honestly didn't know if it was his name mentioned or the fact that

Reggio was a partner of Francesco. At that moment, it was very clear that X didn't know that Reggio was involved in the slaying.

"Whose idea was it to take thirty boys, Francesco?" X piped in with a mean facial expression as she rose upwards to the table and glanced briefly at the large windows.

"I'm going to lay it all out for y'all," Francesco stammered before continuing, "The Esposito's were the only Italians in the United States bringing in top-notch dope from different regions in the world. They needed more workers, which they preferred small hands versus large hands; so Reggio stated that small hands mushed things better than big hands. He knew that Kingston, Jamaica had poor villages and was willing to pay the parents money for "adopting" the boy children, all the while wanting their gems and diamonds. Reggio been had his eyes on that particular village; that's why he vacationed so much out there—to learn the ways of those living out there. That's where you came in, X; you were the mastermind of where the gems and diamonds were located. Your brains helped him find them all and so much more."

Francesco stopped talking and grabbed the glass of water. My patience ran thin, therefore, I knocked the glass of water out of his hand and spat, "Finish, bitch."

Nodding his head as his eyes bulged out, spit sliding from the corners of his mouth, Francesco declared groggily, "Reggio began to extort the poor, nasty village; hoping that they would give into both of his wants—the children and the gems and diamonds. On one of his trips down there, he made a deal with a man; the deal was for Reggio to "adopt" his son in exchange for the man to not owe him money. The man didn't follow through with his son, which pissed Reggio off. In return that one deed pissed off X's uncle, Tyke. Tyke came in and shot the man in his head, took the dude's only son and shoved him in the middle of the dusty street."

Trying not to dip back into that horrible day, I pressed Francesco to continue talking. Quickly glancing at X, the look on her face informed me that she was about to explode from hatred and anger.

"Reggio came up with an idea based on Tyke's action of killing the man and taking the man's only son. Reggio ordered that the families be killed and the thirty boys be taken. That's another aspect in which X came in. She was the one that told us how to get rid of the finger and palm prints, permanently. She dipped the boys' hands in hot tar, cared for the boys' hands, and watched over them on the way back to Miami. Orgon and his brothers had connections within the government; so, they gave Reggio and I birth certificates and social security numbers for the thirty boys taken. Reggio and the Orgon brothers have been in cahoots for two decades. I was introduced to Reggio around the late '90s while I was in the Caribbean Islands looking for quality heroin products. He and I began to do business together heavily once Tyke made X the weapon that he needed her to be. Her ambition to be the best damn queenpin worked wonderfully with our plans."

"So, let me get this correct...the slaying wasn't your idea, but Reggio's?" X asked quizzically.

"Yep. He didn't like for people to tell him no or didn't do what he demanded."

"There's been a shootout in The Parlor. Y'all need to wrap that shit up, now!" Ruger said in my ear, which caused X and me to look at each other. The Parlor was an upscale whore house that Ruger owned, which happened to be the place where Reggio and Dundo were laid up at since the shootout at Ms. Jockton's crib.

"Who burned my family's hut?" I questioned angrily through clenched teeth as I ignored what Ruger said.

"Me," Francesco boasted as he smiled and wobbled from side to side.

"The guards are getting out of the car... kill him now and leave out of the back door. Rondon is in the alley way waiting on y'all in a red Beretta!" Ruger's voice boomed again at the same time X jumped up and walked beside me.

Smack!

Ignoring Ruger once again, I backhanded the shit out of Francesco at the same time X fired off more questions.

"Did you send Juvy's girlfriend a picture of me?"

"Yes," he replied rubbing the right side of his face.

"Why?" she growled.

"Because if I didn't do what Reggio requested, he would've handed the authorities the information on the 2005 slaying, this would have given me the death penalty. I tried to protect you as long as I could, but once he came down here three weeks ago, he wasn't playing this go around. I had to give him what he wanted, which was you... up front and center. I prayed like hell that you caught on to the clues that I was sending you so that you could have a fighting chance."

"Did you know that Tyke wanted me dead?"

"Yes. Why do you think I told you frequently not to trust him? Why do you think I beefed up your security detail?"

"Neither crossed my mind," she spat, looking at me, nodding her head, and walking to the entrance door of the private eating area.

"Get the fuck out of there. Francesco's boys getting out of the car... I'm going to splatter their brains all over the damn pavement," Ruger's deep voice announced through the speakers.

"Okay," X and I replied in unison at the same time I quickly strolled towards Francesco's wobbly body and placed my hand around his neck, which I snapped within seconds.

Within moments of me snapping Francesco's neck, yelling inside of Chivalry took place, and we didn't wait to see how those bodyguards of Francesco's dropped to the ground. I grabbed X's hand and led her through the busy kitchen and out of the back door. Once on foot, we fled like hell toward the getaway car that Rondon was in. After X opened the passenger door, I lifted the lever on the seat and hopped in the back. As she slid her body in the front seat, Rondon was peeling away.

"Is the job handled?" he asked curiously, looking at X.

"Yep."

"Juvy, where are you going?" Rondon asked in a snide tone.

I gave him the address to The Warehouse, where my charcoal Ferrari rested in the back of the building.

"We all still have an issue," X informed us as Rondon drove rapidly along Picktons Avenue.

"Reggio," I said calmly.

"Exactly," she stated as she pulled out her cell phone.

"Ruger, I need you to get me the location on Reggio and Dundo, since there was a shooting at The Parlor."

"We are dropping Juvy off and then we'll be heading to the airport," she quickly, followed by nodding her head.

Before she took the phone from her ear, she spat, "Shit."

At the same time, fuck boy in the driver's seat and I said, "What's wrong?"

"Ruger got word that Reggio and Dundo fled the scene. Five of the six girls are dead, and the one alive have no idea where they're gone."

"Fuck!" Rondon yelled and then continued, "They must die. You need to have a healthy pregnancy, X. I won't have it any other way."

X sat quietly in the front seat with a smirk on her face; I could imagine what she was thinking as her goon/lover talked. Meanwhile, I was in the backseat conflicted and jealous at her for being pregnant by the nigga. For the next six minutes, I was quiet as hell as I waited patiently for fuck boy to pull up in the back of The Warehouse. I welcomed the quietness because my mind had a lot of shit going on. When Rondon pulled up to the back of The Warehouse and parked beside my Ferrari, I wished him and X much success, luck, and congratulated them on their new bundle of joy. Yeah, I was being petty as fuck, and I knew X picked up on it.

After they drove off, I ran toward the inside of The Warehouse where I was greeted by Fish, Bone, and Ms. Jockton as they aimed their weapons at me.

"Well, well, well, Juvian King... it's time for you to die. Everyone that had a direct connection to the 2005 slaying is dead or just about dead," Ms. Jockton stated in a medium-pitched tone.

"Wait! What?... There's no way Bone and Fish are in that mess, so it must be you?" I said lightly, shaking my head.

"It surely is me, Juvy. Reggio Esposito is the father of Bone and Fish. His endeavors are mine, and mine are his," she laughed hysterically before I felt a blunt force to the back of my head and passed out.

Chapter Five

Flema

Saturday, December 9ᵗʰ

Once again, I was looking like a damn fool for Juvy. After I texted him yesterday while at the nail salon about the pregnancy, he responded that after he was done handling some important business, he would stop by so that we could talk. Well hell, it's noon and he still hadn't shown. I didn't bother to text or call his phone. His action told me exactly what he'll be like during the pregnancy.

Ding. Dong.

Now his ass wanna show up, I thought, jumping off the sofa and walking toward the front door.

"Who is it?" I announced, pretending that I didn't know.

"Wilema."

What is she doing here, I thought, unlocking and opening the door.

"Hey, Flema. I just wanted to stop by before I head into work to see did you need anything and to see how you were doing," she stated as she waltzed into my home, wearing a floral pink and blue scrub top, blue bottoms, and a pair of black shoes.

"No, I'm good. I got everything yesterday," I informed her as I motioned for us to walk into the living room.

"Okay," she said lightly and then continued, "How are you feeling?"

"Okay, I guess," I shrugged while taking a seat on the sofa.

Plopping her thick behind beside me, she exhaled heavily. This was the first time that I ever saw my sister distressed and perplexed; not understanding why she would be either of those, I had to see what had her panties in a bunch. Before I said anything, I quickly analyzed her. Curiosity got the best of me, so my nosy tail asked, "What's wrong with you, Sissy?"

"Just tired and stressed."

"Well cut back on the hours and take a vacation. You deserve it, Wilema. You go above and beyond for everyone but yourself."

"True, but I can't afford it right now. I'm getting a house built in Tampa. So, that's taking up my extra funds," she replied, combing through the soft tresses on her head.

"Really? When were you going to tell me?" I inquired happily with a huge smile on my face.

She worked too damn much to be paying someone rent when she could've been a homeowner. I was truly happy for her and everything that she was accomplishing.

"You have so much stuff going on that I didn't want to bore you."

"You'll never bore me, sis. I live through you. You are truly the smart one. You don't let a man get in your way," I said in a matter-of-fact timbre.

Exhaling sharply, Wilema announced, "That's not true. I've been in your shoes and I vowed never to be that person again. That's why I'm very selective in who I give my time too."

Wanting to stretch out, I laid in my sister's lap and began twirling my fingers through my hair. As I toyed with my hair, I gave Wilema my undivided attention. Her eyes were sad and lost. I felt that she needed me to vent; therefore, I was going to return the favor of listening since I've been venting to her since I lost my virginity. Wilema had a story that she wanted to tell me, and my ears were open to hearing her out. Nine times out of ten, there was a message in her speech and I was hungry to know it.

"Who was he?" I asked, eager to know the person that put my sister on high alert with men.

"Juvian King," she stated bluntly as she looked me in the face.

Once Juvy's name came out of her mouth, the look in her eyes changed to hurt and jealousy. I couldn't produce any words as I glared into those eyes of hers. It seemed as if sound and time ceased since it was absolutely quiet in my two-bedroom home. The entire time I looked into my sister's eyes, she stared back into mine, all the while biting down hard on her bottom lip. The way she bit down on her bottom lip told me that she was fighting with herself to not say something that she would regret.

Trying to comprehend when and how she and Juvy became an item, I struggled to get up off her lap so that I could look her in the face. That was until Wilema shoved me back down and held me tightly against her thighs.

"Let me up, Wilema!" I yelped, struggling against my sister's strong hold on me.

"I want to know what's so damn special about you, that he pays for your home and bills. That he makes sure that no one fucks with you... well except the chick that he let whoop the dog shit out of you. Why he's so quick to tell you that he's going to be a father to y'all children, when I clearly had to give up my two children for Fish and Tania to raise," she cried softly as she continued to tightly press her arm against my chest.

Tears slid down my face as I realized that Fish was telling the truth and that my sister lied to me—in my damn face. I felt like the biggest fool as I observed Wilema. At that moment, I wondered did mama know about Juvy and Wilema. I didn't know who I hated the most— Bone, Fish, Tania, Juvy, myself, or my sister. For the past nine years, all of them were in my face, smiling and shit, while holding the most important secret.

"Did mother know about you and Juvy? Why didn't you tell me the truth yesterday when I asked you about the kids?" I sobbed, gazing into her soulless, hurtful brown eyes; the same eyes that made me fight against my sister barricading my body from getting up.

"No, mother doesn't know about Juvy and me. I wanted to tell you the truth, but I didn't expect for you to be pregnant by him. I didn't expect for him to actually care about you more so than me."

"How could you, Wilema... how could you not tell me about you and Juvy? Why have me get involved with him if you and him had a thing going on? How long was it going on? When did it start?" I blurted through tears and a hurt soul.

"I started fucking around with Juvy when he turned seventeen, and he severed all ties between us two months before he left town," she snarled and then continued, "You talking about how could I? How could you? How could you let him get you pregnant and be a father to y'all's child?"

That damn confession took my breath away. All I could do was shake my head and cry even harder. She acted like it was my fault that Juvy didn't want to be with her or have anything to do with the children that they made. I had absolutely no control over that. Hell, she was the one who was fucking my supposed-to-be man!

Shoving me on the floor, Wilema began calling me every name in the book but the child of God. Not wanting to fight my flesh and blood over some dick, I tried to reason with Wilema to leave my home.

"Go to work, Wilema, before we end up saying or doing something that we will regret," I pleaded with my big sister.

"Fuck work, damn it... I'm pissed and hurt, Flema. Somebody gots to pay for how I'm feeling right now!" she screamed as she slapped me across the face.

Backing away from her, I yelled for her to get the hell out of my house. Rushing all of her thickness to me, I was too slow for Wilema and was slammed on the ground. As I rolled over to get up off the floor, Wilema dropped a mean kick to my back which caused me to yelp out from the pain. Struggling to get up from that blow, Wilema screamed, "I hate you!"

"We are sisters, Wilema!" I cried as I raised my body off the ground and rested my head on the gray seats of my sectional.

Wilema grabbed a fistful of my hair and nastily spat, "You will *not* be the mother of Juvy's child. Only I will hold that title!" With a bundle of my hair in her hands, Wilema dragged me toward the rectangular table that sat in the middle of my living room floor and slammed my back against it.

"Ouuch," I sobbed loudly before asking, "Why, Wilema? Why are you going against me for a nigga that clearly doesn't want anything to do with this child? He didn't even show up last night so that we could talk about the pregnancy."

"I hate you!" she spat in my face as spittle landed all over my face.

The first time she said that didn't hurt me as much as this time, because I was looking into her eyes and I knew that she really hated me for something that I didn't do, on top of how Juvy treated her. Those three words she spat at me broke my heart more than finding out about her and Juvy and their children. Not in three centuries would I ever have thought I would hear my sister say that she hated me. While we cried together, I tried to dip into the past to see did they show interest in each other; I couldn't remember one time that I saw either of them giving each other the ogling eye or even carry on a long conversation.

Slowly creeping her hand from my hair down toward my slender neck all the while smiling, Wilema punched me in the throat and that caused me to fight back. As my sister and I tussled all over my living room, I knew it was a live or die moment for my child and myself. I had the best of Wilema until she sent a hard blow to my back, which caused me to fall back on the edge of the rectangular table, causing the back of my head to connect with the hard table. The numbness in my abdomen region came first followed by my legs, and I knew then that I wasn't going to be able to recover from that blow.

Unconsciousness was trying to take ahold of me, but I wouldn't let it; I felt my body being dragged from my living room through the cold hardwood floors of my hallway. There wasn't a damn thing that I could do to defend myself. As I drifted further into the darkness that was calling me, I clearly heard the running water and my sister saying, "I can only imagine how mama is going to cry her eyes out once she's learned that you killed yourself."

No, God, this can't be the end for me. It simply can't be. Please send someone to my home and catch my sister in this horrible act, I thought as I semi-watched my sister peel off my clothing and dump me into the hot water.

It seemed as if my skin was going to peel off. Wanting to cry out, I couldn't; therefore, I cried on the inside. With tears sliding down my caramelized face, I prayed for my soul and asked God to forgive me for my sins. While I was praying with my eyes open, Wilema was nastily glaring at me and praying at the same time.

"If you would've stayed away from him... you would've had a better chance at living," she quickly voiced harshly and then continued, "I'll see you in hell... save a fucking seat for me. Once I get down there, I will try my best to kill your ass again, bitch!"

Struggling to beg my sister not to harm me, I failed miserably. As she submerged my head under the steamy, hot water, I tried to hold my breath as long as I could. Unconsciousness seeped faster along with the water filling my lungs, which got the best of me.

Chapter Six

Rondon

Taking out Francesco and his goons was easy, and I wondered why. There shouldn't have been any reason why that kill was so easy. I really expected to have been in a shootout with them. The entire time X was telling us of her plan, I knew shit was going to get sticky. To my surprise, it didn't and I had to know why; soon as that fuck nigga, Juvy, jumped out of the old, raggedy Beretta that I was driving, I asked my lady, "Why was that kill so easy?"

"Because I made Francesco believe that I wanted to be with him," X sighed as I began to apply pressure on the brakes.

"So, it's not a rumor about you and Francesco, huh?"

"Depends on what the rumor says," she said in a low tone, looking out of the window.

"That you and him were lovers and possibly could still be," I shouted without trying to as I took my foot off the brake and applied it to the gas pedal.

"Not so much as lovers. He was a fuck toy, and I was the one that piqued all of his interest; meaning I could get anything out of him. I didn't see a future with him; hell, I didn't see a future with anyone other than...," her voice trailed off. Without a doubt, I knew who she was talking about and to be quite frank, that shit really angered me. I had to tell myself to calm down since I didn't want to get her riled up.

"Did he ever make your body sing?" I questioned curiously, referring to Francesco.

"Nope, but I made his hiss all types of tunes," she laughed while glancing at me.

This bitch finna make me nut up, I thought while stealing a glance at her.

Ring. Ring. Ring.

"Hello," X said lightly into the phone.

She paused for brief second, and my mind was on trip mode.

"We are on the way now. Go 'head and get things ready for us," she stated casually before saying okay and hanging up the phone.

"To the airport we go?" I inquired.

"Yep."

I wanted to strike up the Francesco lover shit, but it was down the drain as soon as X asked me, "Did you really kill Tyke?"

Without hesitation, I responded proudly, "Hell fuck yes."

"Why?"

"Because Barry froze up and almost shit himself once Tyke upped that tool on him."

"You didn't trust Barry to get the job done?"

"I don't trust anybody when it comes down to you," I told her truthfully.

After that comment, we rode the next ten minutes to Miami International Airport in silence. Grabbing her left hand, it was cold and shaky; it didn't take her long to pull her hand away from mine and place it back into her lap. Once her soft, cinnamon-brown hand connected with the other one, she began to twiddle her thumbs. I wanted to ease her mind, but I just let us be for the moment.

Once I pulled into the parking lot of Miami International Airport, I quickly scanned the area for a deserted parking area. My plan was to dump the car somewhere in the airport's lot where people don't travel much too, far away from other cars. Finding the perfect dump spot, I quickly pulled into it. Before I shut the engine off, X hopped out and waltzed her behind toward the entrance door which was a nice walk. That heifer didn't attempt to say anything to me, and that truly pissed me off. From the time she hopped out until I threw the bomb device in the back seat of the Beretta, I deeply inhaled and exhaled. I didn't stop that breathing technique until I made it upon Ferocious.

I knew X was still pissed at me for throwing up a DNA test. I wanted to know how angry she would get with me, and I swore I didn't think she would be that beasty. Most broads would've whined and cried their damn eyes out all the while slinging shit around the room, to take your head off. Even though she teared up, she still didn't show her ass in the manner I thought she would. I was truly waiting for her to do it so that I could tap that ass—not using my hands though. However, I knew without a doubt that I had to play my cards right, or she would've flatlined my tail.

On the plane the usual shit was going on, J-Money and Baked were smoking a blunt, and Ruger was in the cockpit, as well as X. Ruger and X's bond made me jealous at times because he knew her so well. He was the only one that could calm her down and make her think—well that was unless Tony was involved. Ruger was on X's team before any of us, and I guess that's why they have a special bond; a bond I was trying desperately to steal away from Ruger. X was different with all of us; each of us had our own special thing with her. J-Money and X are into old school cars, so they attended a lot of car shows and watched them on TV. I tried to connect with them on that level, but it was so boring that I had to give it up. Baked and X bonded over food and home improvement stuff. If we didn't have a task to do and were on chill mode, that nigga would get high as a pelican's pussy, tune into a cooking show, and have a helluva meal waiting on one of us to try. He had mad skills in the kitchen; thus him teaching X how to perfect the art of cooking and baking from improving things around the house. Baked was the one that perfected The House of Pain when X brought him into The Savage Clique. He took her vision and turned it into a masterpiece. Baby mother and I bonded over literature, music, and movies.

In school, I was considered a nerd minus the dorky glasses and weird clothing. When I graduated from high school, I had a 4.0 GPA, all advanced courses. I attended college for two years to pursue a degree in something that pleased my father but not me, engineering. I wanted to enter the armed forces, but my mother wasn't hearing that shit at all. Thus, I quickly filled out college applications for anywhere, far away from her controlling ass. I was on the hunt for the perfect life. Not in a million years would I have thought that I would be a wonderful trapper and sniper. I never thought that I would be doing the types of shit I have been doing since I've been connected with The Savage Clique.

"Damn, Rondon, you been quiet since you sat down, you good?" J-Money's deep baritone timbre announced as he took off his black combat boots before fixing his black Dickie pants, ceasing my thoughts.

"Yeah. Just thinking," I replied as I ran my left hand down my face.

"Maneeee, Baked and I were talking about how easy of a kill Francesco and them boys was."

"Yeah, that shit was super easy. You know how Chief do. She gave that nigga a swell conversation," I announced blankly as I looked upwards at the beautiful golden and black marbled ceiling of Ferocious.

The door of the cockpit opened, and we became quiet instantly. Soon as the door opened, I turned my head to see that X had been shedding tears. Her eyes were red and glossy looking. Once she closed the door behind her, she quickly walked past us but I grabbed her right hand at the right time. As I tried to pull her back toward me, she stated nastily, "Know your place, Rondon. I meant what I said, yesterday."

Growing angry, I jumped up and spat just as nasty as she did, "My place? You must've lost your damn mind, X. We made a child together and I'm going to be there... rain, sleet, hail, and snow! Fuck that shit you talking about, on gawd, I'm not hearing that bullshit!"

Clicking her tongue against the roof of her mouth and glaring at me, I knew some fly shit was going to come out of her mouth once she spoke. That heifer just stared at me with the nasty yet bossy 'bitch resting face', as she liked to call it, for a while before she said calmly but sternly, "You know I don't play with folks churren. We ain't in the fucking bedroom. Therefore, you don't run a motherfuckin' thing! Back the fuck up off me and stick to your fucking position like I told you to, *baby daddy!*"

With my hands up, laughing, I replied, "When this motherfuckin' jet touch down in Hope Hull... that ass of yours is mine!"

"Here are The Beast's keys," she responded while tossing them at me and politely walking to the back of the jet, into her personal bedroom.

From the time X and I were semi-arguing, J-Money and Baked were looking amongst the two of us softly chuckling and shaking their heads. Once X slammed the door of the room, Ruger was telling us to buckle up. As we ascended in the air, there was complete silence for at least fifteen minutes. For as long as X had Ferocious, J-Money and Baked were scared of flying, and my petty ass had to laugh and joke on them. Soon as the plane leveled out, the jokesters began with their bullshit.

"Now, how in the hell do y'all suppose to work out? Y'all are too damn stubborn and controlling, and you know Chief is that bitch. Have you actually thought this through?" Baked inquired seriously as he stretched out on the black sofa.

"Shid, that's what I'm saying," J-Money offered his twenty cents into the conversation.

"It'll work out. She's going to be my wife, and y'all ugly asses gonna be in the wedding... tuxedos and all," I said confidently as I closed my eyes.

"That's what's up. Shit, I'm planning the bachelor party," Baked stated before we bust out laughing. That's one cat that knew how to through a damn party, so I didn't have a problem with him throwing me a bachelor party.

Yawning, I slouched down in the soft, black oval chair and thought about how I came to have an interest in X. It was the spring of '07 when I saw her and a strong faced, tall, ancient black nigga, Ruger, strolling through the Valley West Mall in Des Moines, Iowa. She was looking extremely scrumptious as she sashayed through the ivory colored mall, slanging that little, round ass. Her outfit clung to every curve of her body; I wanted to rip that gold shirt, black fitted jeans, and gold thigh high boots off her body and do some strange things to her. Her naturally long, jet-black hair was flowing and bouncing past her shoulders.

I followed her and Ruger throughout the entire mall and was amazed at the thick knot she pulled out in Aéropostale. She had exquisite taste in clothing, shoes, and artifacts. In a gallery store, she paid two thousand dollars for a three piece, handmade African artifact—in which she has the handmade artifact at Safe House Eleven. At first, I thought she was a spoiled brat—like me, until I saw her demeanor change after answering her phone; her once relaxed body was tensed and reeked of aggression. After she announced the word *murder*, she hung up the phone. Upon her hanging up the phone, she and Ruger flew out of the mall, and she was beyond upset. I was hoping that I could get a chance to talk to her, but I never did until three months later when she visited the same mall.

That day was everything because I saw her beautiful smile for the first time, and I loved how her bottom grill shined amongst her perfectly aligned, pearly white teeth. I asked her where she was from, and she replied, "Alabama." Asking the right questions landed me on the website of Alabama State University in Montgomery, Alabama. By the time I turned eighteen, I was in the South attending college.

By August of '07, I was in The Savage Clique, enrolled in six classes at ASU, and lying to my parents. I fell in love with X just by her bossy, demanding yet polite attitude. I fell in love with how she took care of those that showed her loyalty and dedication; her voice pushed me further in love with her. She had a beautiful voice, regardless if she was pissed or not; I loved to hear her sing. I became a conscious being from X. She was always reading eye-opening literature. I learned more of my ancestors' history from the books X provided me than what I was taught throughout my schooling years and parents.

I know I'm not just infatuated with her; I was full blown in love with a woman that loved making and selling large quantities of illegal drugs, and who occasionally assassinated people when the time presented itself. To me, X was more than a vindictive bossy bitch; she was a woman that wanted the finer things in life while dibbling and dabbling on the wild side. With my help, X will be the one she deserves and desires to be, courtesy of my sperm and me being firm with her. She's spoken on many occasions that she wanted to leave the game, but she got sucked back into it. There will be no reasons why she or I will be involved in this life again, once we make sure all ends are tied and burnt. Nothing will come in the way of X being my wife and mother to my children!

After I was done thinking, I hopped up from the chair and ambled toward her private bedroom. Not wasting my time knocking on the ivory-hued door, I slid the door to the right and waltzed in. Laying on her back sideways in the bed, rubbing her stomach all the while listening to music through her Bluetooth earphones, X looked at me and bit down on her bottom lip. Her once angry, frustrated eyes became loving and showed that she was afraid. As I walked closer toward her, she said calmly, "I'm new to all of this, Rondon, and it's going to take me some time to get adjusted. If I hurt your feelings earlier, I'm sorry. I'm re—"

I cut her off by placing my index finger over my mouth and stripping out of my pants. While I was getting naked, X was pulling her dress and thongs off. Opening her legs, I crawled between them and sucked vigorously; the harder I sucked on her thighs, the louder she moaned. "As We Lay" by Kelly Price blared from her earphones, and I made sure to please her until after we landed in Hope Hull.

The plane was on the ground and the fellas were gone by the time we were finished. Before dressing myself, I dressed my woman with a proud heart and a smile on my face, until she mentioned my mother.

"What will your mother think about you getting me pregnant?"

It was no secret that my mother didn't like X. Whenever my family visited Alabama, my mother let it be known that she didn't care to be around X. On the other hand, my father and brothers loved her.

"She'll be excited," I lied, not looking at her while putting on my clothes and boots.

"Tell me the truth. Don't ever lie to me, Reginald."

"Okay, I'm sorry. My mother will be alright. Either she'll get on board, or she'll miss out on being a grandmother," I explained tightening up my belt before picking my woman up and exiting the plane.

"If you say so."

Letting that conversation go while locking the door on Ferocious, I informed X to get in the passenger seat of The Beast. Once I made sure that Ferocious was good and locked down, I jogged to X's black trimmed in gold Caprice as she opened the driver's door for me.

With a wide grin on my face, I thought as I slid into the front seat, *Yes, she really feeling a nigga more than she did Tony. She never opened the door for him.* Peeling away from the large estate, she brought up the pregnancy and I didn't mind one bit.

"You can back out you know, and I won't kill you," she said in a low tone.

"Back out for what? What did I tell you when we first fucked and I didn't pull out of you?" I stated sternly.

"I know. I just don't want... nevermind."

"I'm glad that you stopped that part of the conversation. X, look, I've been wanting to be in your life as your man since I first placed my eyes on you back in the spring of '07. I prayed day in and out that I would get the chance to meet you again. Guess what? I did, and on top of that, I did everything in my power to be around you, constantly. So that I could protect you all the while learning everything about you. I'm not going anywhere, regardless who the fuck doesn't like it. They can get murdered, just like that!" I stated sternly while glancing at her as I sped down I-65 North.

"Okay... hmm," she stammered while twiddling her thumbs and then continued, "I'll schedule an appointment first thing Monday, morning."

"Alright. I'm going to be at all doctor's appointments and parenting classes, understand?"

"Yes."

"Where are we staying tonight?" I asked, hoping she was going to say in the country.

"At Safe House Eleven."

What a wonderful night this is going to be, I sang in my head as I proceeded to jump on Highway 80, heading toward Jones, Alabama. As I drove past Big Lots distribution center, X picked up her phone and pressed and held down on the number two; I knew then that she was calling Ruger. Within seconds she spoke in a tired voice, "Ruger, go to The House of Pain and let Tony go… tell him if he really values his life and that of his family, he would keep his motherfucking mouth shut about all that he witnessed and what happened to him. Call me when you drop him off in the middle of the Eastern Boulevard."

Right then, I knew that X lost her fucking mind. Tony saw too much shit to live. I was fuming as she told Ruger to let the nigga go, but I wasn't going to voice my opinion. It was time for me to get her the fuck off the throne before she fucked around and landed herself in prison for life. There was no way in hell that I was going to raise my child without her; there was no way in hell that I was going to live one day without X'Zeryka Nicole Toole. Tony's ass had to die before I let him sing one damn word to the Fed's or any other law enforcement agency.

***

X and I had watched the fourth installment of Hidden Colors, ate good, and were laid back on her cream and gold cotton sofa, soaking up knowledge. My baby was tired since I kept pausing the documentary to get up inside of her; before we decided to watch

TV, I was murdering her for talking slick out the mouth. She was going to learn that I was not playing with that ass, not even on that street tip no more. With her in the crook of my left arm, I glanced at the DVR box for the time, and it read 8:30 p.m. It was time for me to call my parents to check on them and to deliver the good news. Even though I knew my mother was going to say some shit that pissed me off, I had to mentally and physically prepare myself. I really wanted her involved in my child's life. Therefore, I said a long silent prayer before picking my phone up and dialing my parent's home phone.

On the third ring my father, Jetson Martin, answered the phone, "Hello, there, son. How are you?"

"I'm good, Dad. How are you?" I asked rubbing X's arm, gently.

"Good minus having a disturbing day on the job, but anywho... what's going on?"

"Nothing much. Had the day off, so I enjoyed to the fullest," I lied. My folks still thought I was doing graphic design for rappers and singers, an obvious lie I told them.

"Son, you are still young and talented... I really wish--," he began to say but quickly cut it short and changed his entire speech, "Uggh... Reginald... I'm glad that you enjoyed your off day."

I was glad that he changed the subject; I just started talking back to him. Months ago, he decided that he wanted to say the wrong shit to me, and I wasn't up for hearing it. My life is just that, my fucking life. How I wanted to live was my business. Who I wanted in it was my business. I was tired of them on that fuck style shit. At first, it was my mother always dictating what and who I did, and then my father started on the shit. A nigga grew tired of it real quick!

"Thanks, Dad," I replied sheepishly, already wanting to hang up the phone that was until my mother hopped on the phone, with that annoying, fake ass tone.

"Reginald, darling, how are you?"

"Fine, Mom, how are you?"

"Great. When are you coming up to visit?"

"For Christmas. Me and X'Zeryka are coming up," I stated happily, looking down at the beauty that was falling asleep.

"That's great, Son. Tell her we are excited to see her," my father's voice boomed through the phone, overpowering my mother's response, which I didn't hear clearly.

That damn woman made sure that her statement was heard, "Reginald, you know how I feel about that woman. She is not welcome here, and I meant that!"

"Now, Regina, you will not put me in this mess of yours. I see nothing wrong with X'Zeryka," my father spoke sternly to my mother.

"Well, Mom you won't have to worry about seeing me, then, and you surely don't have to worry about being a grandmother to my child!" I spat angrily, fire building up inside.

"I'm going to be a grandfather!" my father yelled excitedly at the same time my mother replied nastily, "With that woman?"

My mother's response killed me ten times over, I wanted to reach through the phone and choke her ass clean out! That's how pissed I was. I quickly slid my body away from X, since I didn't want to wake her as I argued with my mother. Quickly and quietly, I placed a white blanket over X. I was eager to curse my mother out as I had to endure the hateful words she spat about my woman to my dad. They argued from the time my mother spoke until I walked in the front yard and fired up my cigarette.

"Enough!" I spat in a demanding tone.

"Who are you talking to like that, Reginald?" my mother hollered in the phone.

"You mostly, Mom. I'm a grown man, and I make my own choices in life. You can't respect anything that I do. I'm not going to be an engineer so get over it. I'm not going to marry Jessica Motley, so get over it," I commanded as I inhaled my cigarette.

"Don't make me get ghetto on your ass, Reginald Rondon Martin. I think I will have to since that's the type of shit you like... ghetto, money hungry, gold digging bitches!" my mother snapped, which made me start growling.

"Son, calm down, please. Regina, you know you are showing your entire ass," my father stated as I growled louder followed by howling.

"What in the fuck is wrong with this boy?" my mother asked quizzically.

"I'm pissed the fuck off and I want to kill!" I told her and I meant every damn word. The line went quiet and I continued to hold the phone to my ear to hear what in the hell was going to be said next by my mother. My father was learning to stay out of my business and to be happy for me, and for the life of me, I couldn't figure out why my mother couldn't do the same thing.

With a more pleasant tone, my mother stated, "There's something about her son that I don't like."

"The first time I saw X'Zeryka, I thought the same thing. However, one conversation with her changed my entire view. She's intelligent, and to be frank with you Mom, X'Zeryka is way smarter than you. She holds a lot of degrees from top notch schools. So, get to know her first before trying to judge, and you and I will be alright. You will love her just like dad, Roger, and Ronald do," I confessed lightly as I tried to change the pitch of my tone, which was riled back up after her response.

"I'm assuming she's the one that your dumb ass got pregnant, huh? Don't answer but hear me loud and clear, if you don't make her have an abortion, I will cut your inheritance completely off. I didn't raise you to fall for those types of girls. Gold diggers... money hungry hoes, Reginald Rondon Martin. Do I make myself clear?"

Laughing loudly before snapping, "Mom, fuck your money... if you were as smart as you said you are... you would've known that I sent that money right back to the account you sent it from! I make my own money... you must think I'm Ronald and Roger. I like my own money with no stipulations on how to live my life. Until you get your mind right, you won't be hearing from me."

"You know what happens when you don't do what I ask of you. Don't you?" she inquired, not caring about what I said to her.

"Yes, ma'am, but you don't know what will happen if you don't listen to me," I spat back.

"And this one here is no different. Do not test me, Reginald," she breathed in a low tone, still ignoring my threats.

"Keep acting like you don't hear me, Regina! Matter of fact, fuck keep talking to you!" I replied angrily and sternly before hanging up the phone in their faces.

Tread lightly, Mother. Tread lightly, I thought as I fired up another cigarette all the while, dialing Ruger's number.

Chapter Seven

Tony

I didn't know what time it was when the back door of the barn opened, but I knew it was nighttime since it was completely dark outside. The cold air rushed inside and I was thankful. I thought a barn was supposed to have been cold, but this motherfucker was hot!

"I'm here to release you. You can't get in my whip stinking it up. Once you take a bath, I'm driving you to Montgomery and dropping you off. You will *not* tell anyone what you have witnessed or what has happened to you, understand?" Ruger said as he started walking toward me with clothes slung over his right shoulder.

"Yes, I understand," I said gratefully. At that moment, my heart was filled with joy to the point I wanted to cry.

"Good," he replied as he unlocked the bolts from around my ankles, followed by my wrists.

Thank you, God, for watching over me, I sang in my head as Ruger motioned for me to get to the bathroom while handing me the clothes that were hung over his shoulder. I welcomed the bathroom with a smile on my face; I was very grateful that X allowed me to live. However, I was disappointed that she didn't release me herself. I wanted to apologize to her for how I hurt her, thank her for letting me go, and tell her that I forgive her. True enough I should've been pissed at her for the treatment she told DB to render me; I asked God to help me overcome that, which he granted.

Turning on the water knobs, I awaited the steams before jumping in. It didn't take long for the water to get toasty, the way I liked; Hopping in, I let the hot water bless my body before washing. Quickly washing my body, I thought about the smiles that my family would have on their faces when they saw me. Two images of my family caused me to cut my bath short and put on the clothes that Ruger handed me.

Before I knew it, I shouted, "Thank you, Jesus. It was all you!"

After I was done thanking the Man above, I opened the bathroom door to a clean pair of socks and my old shoes, sitting in the middle of the floor. Putting them on, I began to feel anxious. The palms of my hands were sweaty and my throat felt clammy as I strolled toward the place I'd been held captive at.

"Ruger, I'm ready," I stated happily in a high-pitched tone.

"Very well then. Let's hit the road," he responded, walking toward the back door as I ran out of it; hoping X wasn't going to call him and change the plan.

Within four minutes, I was away from the barn that held me and my spirits at an all-time low. On the long drive back to my native city, my mind was all over the place. I knew the questions were going to come from my family; however, I had a plan for all of that. The only thing I was going to tell them was that I had to get away from the stressors of life; they should buy that. It would make me look like the bad person, but oh well; I was going to keep my word that I wasn't going to say anything.

All my family was going to do was spread rumors, and I was okay with that. My main concern was the safety and well-being of my children. They were the reason why I prayed so hard and decided to give my life over to Jesus. After the unconditional love he's shown me since I was at that barn place, I had no choice but to serve him.

"Why would you betray her?" Ruger asked out of the midst of nowhere, while we were in the middle of nowhere.

"I didn't want to. I begged Gorilla to leave me alone," I stated nervously.

"You were fucking with the most powerful woman in the world. You didn't think she would protect you and your children?" he questioned as he slid through the curved road.

Through clenched teeth, Ruger continued, "That woman would've gone to hell and back for you."

Feeling low for not coming to X when Gorilla approached me, I sighed heavy and shook my head.

"Did you even love her?"

"Yes," I replied, looking at Ruger's body language.

"I can't tell. You know why I didn't want her fucking with you?" he growled.

"Why?"

"Because she is simply too fucking good for you... minus the dope making and selling and killing. She's brilliant and deserved way more than what she was getting from whatever y'all had going on."

"I know."

"Obviously not," he said blankly as he began to break speed for the stop sign that lie ahead on County Road One.

As I thought about what Ruger said, he fired up a cigarette and rolled down the window. He began to hum at the same time the passenger door opened. Quickly turning my head toward the passenger door, I stared at a smiling-faced Rondon and his gun. I was truly shell-shocked by seeing that nigga and wondering where in the fuck he came from, that was until I felt a gun to the back of my head.

"I was actually going to let you go as Chief requested, but then Rondon brought to my attention that she's full of hormones and shit... since she's pregnant and all. I had to step in and make sure that *our* Chief will be absolutely fine! No death penalty will be brought against her... able to raise her baby with Rondon... a fucking normal life is what she will have!" That was the last thing that I heard before blackness occurred.

Chapter Eight

X

Sunday, December 10th

It was a gorgeous, beautiful, warm day and it just so happened to be the day of Truk's burial; all of the family, close associates of Truk, and of course myself and remaining goons showed up to show their final respects. As the funeral took place, I was zoned out; I didn't want to be in that motherfucker in the first place. Showing respects to a nothing ass nigga was not my thing; however, this wasn't my first rodeo of a charade.

Auntie Julia was all over the damn floor as she raised her hands toward Truk's gold and black urn, while hollering and carrying on. Damn wig fell off, and I was the only one laughing. Rondon nudged me; I briefly looked at him nastily and turned my head back to the circus show that was going on in front of me.

After the puny ass funeral finished, a scrawny ass dude carried Truk's urn out of the church, I don't know what dude had going on, but that nigga dropped the damn urn, in the front of the church doors. As soon as the urn hit the grown and splattered, screams spilled out of everyone's mouths except mine and my crew. When I say that my ignorant, pregnant, no manners having ass was out there laughing, I was. Auntie Julia was hollering and cussing the dude out something awful. As she cursed and dropped to her knees trying to scoop up her son's ashes, I had tears coming down my face while others were shaking their head at what took place. I didn't stop laughing until Rondon rushed me off the church grounds, toward the gravel parking lot across the street from the church.

"You so wrong for laughing, baby," he told me before he closed the passenger door on The Beast.

Not paying his ass any attention, I looked at the crowd of people and shook my head. Opening the driver's door, Rondon hopped in and started the engine. With nothing to say to him, I turned on the radio, but he cut it off.

"Why are you doing that?"

"You are not going to beat the block down, X," he said sternly.

With a frown on my face, I spat, "I'm semi-heartless yes, but careless... never that."

Sighing heavily, he made sure that the radio knob was turned down before he cut my device back on and turned off the amps. Not in the mood to tell him a piece of my mind, I sat my behind back in the seat and waited for the charade games to be over.

Chapman Cemetery was literally two minutes away from the church, but it took us at least twenty minutes before we left the church. I had to see why in the hell it was taking so long for us to leave. When I did ask, some blonde-headed, dark-skinned chick told me that they were sweeping up Truk's ashes and putting it into a box. Five minutes after she told me that, we were heading to the cemetery. Upon the entrance into the cemetery, I began to feel sad. My grandmother was buried at the same place we were getting ready to place Truk's ashes. Ready to get this day over with, I hopped out of the car and avoided looking at my grandmother's final resting place. With my guys by my side, we heard the preacher talking about some salvation. Caring not to hear any more of his words, I tuned him out.

Thoughts of my grandmother appeared and flooded through my brain, causing me to grow angry at the fact that she was no longer living. Another fact that made me upset was that I still didn't know who was responsible for shooting up her home. Doing away with Truk's burial site, I walked over to my grandmother's final resting place. Rondon, Ruger, Baked, and J-Money knew where I was going, yet they didn't bother me; however, they did keep a close eye on me. Upon approaching my grandmother's grave, I felt the warm tears racing down my cinnamon-brown face; I felt my body breaking down, down to the ground as I rubbed her warm cement tombstone.

Crying, I said softly, "Grandma, I'm sorry I didn't listen to you. I wish I could turn the hands of time back and do it all over again. The material possessions that I have are nothing, especially when I don't have you. I'm ready to change and I need your help to watch over me and my guys. I'm ready for a family, I'm ready for love, and I'm ready to be someone's wife... well not just anyone, but the one that's growing on me... well, that I'm pregnant by rather... I suppose."

A soft kiss was planted on the right side of my neck as the body of the man I've been lying with cradled my petite body in his arms. While I finished talking, my other fellas came over to my grandmother's grave and paid their respects. Slowly getting up, Rondon held out his left hand for me to take. Placing my hand in his and turning around, he wiped my tears away. Before I left my grandmother's gravesite, I blew a kiss and told her that I'll always love her. I held my head high and smiled that lovely, bright smile that my grandmother loved oh so much.

"Are we even entering this repast bullshit?" J-Money questioned curiously.

"Hell yeah, I'm finna eat my money up," I chuckled as they began to laugh.

"Mane, you are wild," Baked stated quickly and then continued, "What you got catered there?"

"A variety of Publix food, Panera Bread, Papa Johns, and some soul food from Mr. Brown's place," I replied as my stomach began to rumble.

"Hell yeah, we finna eat this damn food up. We... well, the fellas finna get high and fuck up all that good shit you don' paid for," J-Money joked while the others agreed.

I had a severe pouting facial expression at the mention of them getting high. Rondon quickly addressed my facial expression by saying sternly, "Fix yo' damn face!"

If those fool heads of mine didn't bust out laughing in the middle of the cemetery and had folks looking at us, then I don't know who did. I was about to say something smart to his ass until he nipped it in the bud, "Baby, I was practicing before the baby get here. You know Daddy gotta be stern."

Chuckling while shaking my head and walking off, I held up my index finger.

"What that mean?" he asked as he hit the unlock and auto start buttons on my whip.

"Strike one," I replied, turning around and seductively licking my lips.

"Shit... I'mma strike out then since it's going to be like that."

"Save that shit to after this repast, man... a nigga wanna laugh, flirt with the dusties that got on them damn jelly shoes with a dirty mop head plastered on their skulls," Baked shouted. At his comment, I almost pissed on myself.

I have never heard of no bullshit like that before, and then the other fools started clowning on the batches of sea bitches in horrible outfits that attended the funeral and burial site. I was weak from laughter as I climbed in the passenger seat.

"Let's go now. I got plans for the night... chop chop," I told them while trying to tone down the laughter.

"Yes, Chief," they replied in unison, but that damn Rondon put his own little twist to Chief—it had me real wet!

After we made it to the cars we were riding in, we peeled off to Auntie Julia's house. She hadn't left the burial site yet, but I was sure some old heads were at her house. The ride to Auntie Julia's house was very interesting; Rondon slipped his fingers in between my legs. I caught a wonderful nut while he was driving, and that guy was ready to head back to Safe House Eleven, but I told him no.

As Rondon pulled The Beast into my aunt's small front yard, I sighed heavily before welcoming the fuckery from my ugly ass mother's presence! Rondon asked me was I okay, and I replied, "As ever." I wanted to wait until more people arrived at Auntie Julia's house before I hopped out of the car. Ten minutes later, I slid my body out of The Beast. For the one-hundredth time when in the presence of anyone, all eyes were on us. With a smile and a Miss America wave, those eyes got the fuck off us, and my goons started laughing—as usual. I saw more people than I could of the house itself; that's just how small Auntie Julia little ass shack was. With nowhere to sit, I told Rondon to put me on the hood of the car and of course, it was done. As I was chatting with my guys on some non-serious shit, one of my most likable cousins, Keithia, strolled toward my car with a huge smile on her face.

Keithia shouted, "Hey, cousin!"

What's up, lady?" I stated happily as I observed her appearance. She stood five foot five, around 130 pounds, dark-skinned, small brown glasses that were pushed on the bridge of her nose, and petite titties and butt. Keithia was rocking the hell out of a green short sleeve shirt, denim tight fitting jeans, and a pair of green booties; the gold accessories popped the green off just the right way. Black and burgundy weave flowed flawlessly into a jagged bob, which was feathered on the sides.

"Shit, hiding from my mama. I don't want her to see me high," she giggled as I shook my head while laughing.

"You already know mama ain't playing 'bout that weed shit. I'm surprised you ain't facing one," Keithia stated in a matter-of-fact tone.

"Nope... The Kid pregnant, yo," I said, rubbing on my knee.

"Are you fucking serious bitch?" she asked, placing her hand over her mouth.

"Yeah," I laughed, finally feeling okay with the fact that I was having a baby with Rondon.

"I'm so happy for you... congratulations, cousin," she piped as she opened her arms, causing me to lean into them.

"Thank you."

"I da' pappy," Rondon shouted, with his eavesdropping ass.

That silly fool had all of us laughing as he imitated Bernie Mac from *Life*.

"Why your crew so damn goofy, X?" she inquired while laughing.

"I have no idea, but he's telling the truth."

"Well... shit we gotta catch up baddd."

"Indeed. Anywho, you looking good girl," I told her with a pleasant smile as I saw the batches of bad ass kids running and yelling around in the yard.

"Thank you. You already know you doing the damn thing. Girl, please donate me some of that ass," she joked with a huge smile on her face. I couldn't help but laugh because the way she had her lips puckered was hilarious.

"Yo' ass look very delicious in those denim jeans," J-Money said to Keithia.

"Why, thank you, sir," she replied as she batted her eyes.

"You are mighty handsome in your unusual attire, J-Money," Keithia piped as she observed him in a black, fitted suit.

After they were done complimenting each other, Keithia resumed the conversation of wanting me to donate some ass to her. That entire conversation had me tickled to the max. I knew exactly what she was doing—getting me happy before my sorry ass mammie tried to rain on my parade.

"Nih, cuz... you know I need all this ass," I stated, rubbing on my juicy bottom that sat high on my back. No lie, I had ass for days. It was rounded and stood at attention. That thang would hypnotize men if they stared at it too long while it was in rotation.

"That's why yo' ass pregnant nih... throwing that shit in rotation... off the banister... in the club stuntin' and shit," Baked joked, which caused my goons, Keithia, and myself to bust out laughing.

She and I chit chatted a while before we decided to walked inside of the house to speak to everyone. Once I made it to the front porch, I felt like I was in a damn campaign: shaking hands, speaking, greeting, meeting new people, and smiling. I thought I was going to be able to do small talk and keep it moving, but it didn't work out like that. I finally made it to my destination—the kitchen and wished I stopped at the living room. At the family table sat none other than Shunda Toole, my mother. She was looking at me like I was the most disgusting thing on Earth, and I looked at the bitch the same damn way. I spoke to everyone but her and turned around quickly.

"I'm surprised you showed up," Shunda snickered as she clapped her brown hands together.

"Don't start no shit and I won't have to shoot this bitch up, Shunda. Y'all have a nice time," I said loudly while turning around to face the girl that gave birth to me.

In my eyes, Shunda will always be a girl to me. She would never grow up and be a woman. She was stuck on a dick that didn't want her or me; thus leaving me with my grandmother.

"Now, Shunda and X, we are not about to do this shit today," Keithia said softly while grasping my hand.

"Hey, little lady. How are you today?" one of my grandmother's friend, Ms. Nancy, said politely as she walked from the cramped, small hallway.

"Good. How are you?" I asked Ms. Nancy sweetly.

"I'm fine. You been M.I.A lately. What you been up too?" she asked while opening her arms and wiggling her short, fat light-skinned fingers for me to come to her.

"Making and selling drugs," Shunda spat nastily.

I growled and cocked my head to the side. I was about to open my mouth until Ms. Nancy stepped in.

"X'Zeryka is your first-born child. Why must you be so evil toward her? If you can't say anything nice, then don't say shit at all!" Ms. Nancy barked at the egg donor.

"Whew, let me get out of here. The hostility in here is too much for me, especially when there isn't one person in this room that took care of me because they were too busy running behind the male species that didn't want their tired, broke-down, no goals, no money, bouncing from house to house, no ambition having ass," I laughed wickedly as I stared at Shunda.

Leaving my vindictive ways alone, I became serious as I kissed Ms. Nancy on the right side of her cheek.

I jetted out the front door and came to a complete stop once I saw Rondon, licking his damn lips. He was looking absolutely delicious in a black collar short sleeved shirt, denim jeans, black Timberland boots, and a fitted black hat. A gold necklace around his slender chocolaty neck, a gold ring on his right pinky finger, a gold watch on his right wrist, and those damn gold teeth were sparkling; his waves were making me seasick but had me ready to run my hands through them. My pussy started doing numbers!

"X! Guh, what's wrong with you?" Keithia laughed. That caused everybody to turn and look at me—including Rondon. My slick ass was on game as soon as she said my name. I told her that I was looking like that because of something that I heard from inside the living room; I wasn't ready for everyone to know about me and Rondon yet.

He glared at me and licked them got damn lips, if I didn't hightail it off that porch then I don't know what I did. I hit the button on my keypad to start my speakers to talking. The beat of "Vampires and Mirrors" by Wickett and King South dropped, and the females, including myself, went insane when the hook came in. All I heard was, "*I want cha! I need cha! In the mirror! I see ya! I like the way you move!*" Titties bouncing, pussy popping, ass shaking, noisy drunk bitches equaled a massive dancing contest. Even I got in on the action. I became extra and danced my ass off. Rondon's ass stood back and watched, but by the time that "Rock It" by Master P and 5th Ward Weebie played, he was right behind me as I was winding my body along to the beat.

An hour later, my fam and I danced, drank, ate, rapped, sung, and chatted. After I finished my fifth plate in the driver's seat of my whip, I was ready to go; especially when I saw Rondon walking behind my car followed by him tapping on the passenger side window, I unlocked the door, and he hopped in. The nigga didn't ask me any questions as he gently shoved me against the driver's door and gave me a kiss out of this world. The kiss he planted on my lips had me shaking and begging for him to continue, which he did. Things were getting real hot and heavy until Keithia opened the back driver's side passenger door.

"Oh shit, my bad," she said apologetically, eyes bucked and left hand covering her mouth before she closed the door.

Rondon and I fell silent as he stared at me while sliding his tongue across both of my nipples. I groaned and he chuckled. After I play hit him, he straightened up my shirt and bra, which were over my head at the time Keithia opened the door. He glanced at me, shrugged his shoulders and said, "Well, we are going to my house."

"I want you now, Rondon," I whined while grasping his beautifully sculpted chest.

"I want you too. Go to my house," he demanded as he rubbed the back of my right hand.

Pulling away from my Aunt's house, I tooted the horn and got the fuck out of the way. By the time I got to the end of the dusty rocky road, my phone began to ring. Looking down at the screen at the unfamiliar number, I answered in a boss-like manner, "Talk to me."

"I'm coming for you," Bango stated before hanging up the phone.

"Rondon, that was Bango...get Ruger, J-Money, and Baked on my ass now... he said that he is coming for me," I told him bossing all the way the fuck up!

As he called and informed Ruger of what Bango said to me, I reached in the back seat to grab my PX-4 and sawed-off shotgun. Looking in the mirror, I saw my goons were right behind me. Upon seeing the Tahoe, I fled from Happy Hollow, down the steep hill and briefly stopped at the stop sign. Pushing the gas pedal to the floor, I hauled ass while Rondon was suiting and booting his choice of weapon.

As I approached the stop sign on East Sixth Street in Prattville, I saw a silver Yukon not slowing down; therefore, I sped up hoping that I would escape the collision, which I did but not before I hollered, "Bango!" Rondon was already out of the window slanging a hand grenade, while Ruger, Baked, and J-Money, in the

Tahoe behind me, starting shooting toward the silver SUV. Big holes ripped through the sides, windows, and tires, which caused the truck to flip over on the driver's side.

"Get the fuck out of the city now, X. The country we go!" Rondon stated sternly as I took my eyes off the scene behind me.

If I would've had my eyes focused on the road, I would've seen the all-black F-250, coming straight toward us. There was no way I could completely avoid the collision, so I decided to make a swift left turn; aiming for someone's backyard, that had a deep ditch some feet away from the back porch. The front end of the F-250 caught the backend of The Beast and spun that motherfucker around. In the process of being hit hard, I banged my head on the steering wheel at the same time Rondon said "shit" followed by calling my name.

"X!!!!" I heard Rondon saying through the blasting of gunfire, which I tried to see who was shooting but my head and nose were hurting badly.

"I'm okay. I'm okay. Get us the fuck out of here by taking control over the steering wheel," I told him as he grabbed my PX-4 and began shooting, through my damn front windshield! At the moment, I couldn't be mad, but I knew I would be. The gunfire ceased and all I heard was Ruger's deep voice.

"Rondon, the coast his clear. Get Chief the fuck out of here! I'm going to set the truck on fire," Ruger yelled from behind my car.

"A'ight... meet us at S.H.E.," Rondon spat loudly, which was code for Safe House Eleven. The only time we said S.H.E. was in the public where anyone could be listening.

As he quickly placed me in the passenger seat, he jumped in the driver's seat, and hauled ass back toward Northington Street. He made a smart choice of going in a complete loop to avoid the police since it was plausible that they would be coming from the direction that was closer for us to get the hell out of the city; I didn't have time to explain shit to them. Even though they were on my payroll, I still had to at least act like a law-abiding citizen. Halfway up Northington Street, there was a black Dodge Ram truck that was flying down the middle of the road.

"Trouble lies ahead and I'm finna air it the fuck out!" I yelled as I grabbed my sawed-off shotgun.

After I rolled down the window, I cocked it back and start letting it loose, as I was hanging out of the window. Aiming for the tires and windows simultaneously, I fucked up the Dodge Ram with the help of my goons, who were behind me. Before long, the Dodge Ram plummeted into a tree in front of someone's yard. With a growing crowd standing on their porches looking at the chaos, Rondon fled the scene.

"Bango got his people's coming from all angles," Rondon spoke at the same time my cell phone rang.

Looking down to see who was calling me, I quickly slid my hands on the answer button as Ruger's name appeared on my screen.

"Talk to me," I ushered blankly.

"Reggio's men are strong on our asses. You need to flee to Safe House Six. I've already called and ordered everyone to get out. We are heading down to Safe House Eleven and scope shit out."

"Okay."

"Be safe, X," Ruger said sincerely before I told him and the others to be safe and report to me soon as they could.

After I hung up the phone, I told Rondon where to go and drop off The Beast; there was no need in driving an hour and fifty minutes in a damaged 'hot' car—that equaled a disaster. Stopping by a hideaway spot on the opposite end of Camellia Estates, we dropped my first love and hopped in my silver 2016 Honda Accord. Once on the road, my adrenaline slowed down and I was able to think. My thoughts led me to the one person that caused me to feel love; the one person that took my virginity and truly had me thinking that love was a joke in this industry, Bango.

"X?" Bango whispered as he rubbed my shaking thigh.

"Yes," I said lightly as I looked into his hazel-greenish eyes.

"May I taste you?"

"What do you mean?" I asked, fumbling with my hands and avoiding eye contact.

Getting on his knees at the same time he tapped lightly on my private, I shook until I couldn't anymore. I was nervous about the action that he wanted to do. I was scared out of my mind because I knew that I felt more for him than what I should. My mind was telling me to push him off me, but my heart and body craved him. Planting my brown eyes on his face, I slowly nodded my head—giving him the go ahead to taste me. As he took off my shorts followed by my panties, he told me to lay back on his bed and open my legs. For God knows how long, I was in pure bliss as he took his time tasting and pleasing me.

That day shouldn't have happened because in reality, it did make me vulnerable to him; if I would've stopped what took place between us then I wouldn't be in the position that I was in, as we speak. I would've never sent out the hit to scare Taea. I hated that bitch with a passion; I envied her because she had the one that I wanted in my life. She had the free will to be with Bango, or any man, and I didn't—all because of who my uncle and I wanted to be.

I knew that I had to ask myself, Taea, and Bango to forgive me. In order for me to live a happy life with Rondon by my side, I knew I had to right my wrongs with the first person that I never meant to hurt, Bango, in hopes that I am able to live a crime-free life.

#

Taea

I was tired of waiting on Bango to cease that bitch, X. She was the reason why my wedding went to shits in a matter of minutes, a year ago. She was the reason why I was raped and beaten; she was the reason why I couldn't sleep at night. That whore had to die! I was never the type to fight over Bango, but I'll be damned if a bitch was going to come on my territory and destroy it. Ever since Bango and I came into this world, bitches and niggas been picking a fight with me about him, and I was plain damn tired of it. It was time for me to take matters into my own hands, since Bango was taking his precious time in getting rid of the bitch.

"Where are you finna go?" he asked as he rubbed my back.

"Out for a drive. I need to clear my head. I'm ready to blow on your motherfucking ass," I stated nonchalantly as I turned around to stare my husband in the face.

"Stay in your place, Taea. Don't go fucking with no one that you aren't ready for," he said for the one-hundredth time this week.

Growing angry at his response as if I was a weak bitch, I exploded at his comment. "What the fuck? Do you think I'm weak or something? Do you think I can't handle my own? I'm a grown ass woman who can handle her own front... know that nigga!"

Roughly pulling me down on his childhood bed, Bango got on top of me and stared me in the face. Something wasn't right, and I knew it. There was a reason why he pussyfooted with knocking the bitch off, and I was not going to have her living one second longer.

"I'm the man, and I'm going to make all the moves. Do you understand that?" he said sternly as he stared into my eyes.

"No, I don't. You had numerous chances to knock the bitch off and you didn't! Why, Bango, why?" I said loudly as tears rolled down my face.

"Taea Johnson, leave that shit alone!" he barked, getting his tall, light-skinned body off me as his phone rang.

Ready to get to the bottom of the shit, I hopped off the bed and ran behind him as he reached for his phone, which I knocked on the floor before pushing him.

"You are my fucking husband whom was shot on our wedding day! You are going to tell me why in the fuck, you didn't kill that bitch when we saw her in Miami, Bango!"

Sighing heavily, Bango looked at me and said, "Because I couldn't. I have some questions for her. I really feel like she didn't mean to shoot me."

"That's a motherfucking lie! The bitch came for you and clearly stated your damn name. How in the fuck she didn't mean to shoot you?" I asked with an attitude as I placed my hands on my hip.

"I know her all too well, Taea. I know her. Plus, I learned of some information that made my suspicions valid." His voice trailed off as he looked at the ground.

"Look at me when you are talking to me damn it. Have you fucked the bitch before? Were you in a relationship with her?"

"Yes, I had sexual intercourse with her before... when we were younger up until what Rodrigo did to you. We were never in a relationship because she wouldn't allow it," he confessed as he looked at me.

Smack!

After I slapped his face, I stormed out of his childhood room, which was at his grandmother, Toot's, home. On my ass while I stomped down the hallway, Bango called after me. Ignoring him, I kept on about my business. I was determined more than ever to get to the bitch! She was not going to threaten my home because she wanted him! He was mine and mine alone! I was not going to have her breathing, knowing that they had history!

Shoving me into Grandma Toot's large, brown kitchen table, and turning me around, Bango pressed his face closely to mine and spat, "Do not take your ass to Prattville or ask anyone to call upon X. The last thing I need you to do is get out in these streets and act like you are a boss bitch! You are not! Don't go fucking with someone that's not in your league!"

"Fuck you, Bango! I do as I please! I will not have a bitch threatening my home, family, and testing my gangsta, point blank period."

"Taea, you are really pissing me the fuck off! I wish you would listen to me this one time. You are going to fuck around and get yourself killed, and I can't have that on my conscience. I need you in my life. I need you to trust me. Baby, please trust me."

"Let me go so that I can get the hell away from you. I'm liable to tell you something that you don't want to hear, and once it comes out of my mouth... you know I will follow through with it!"

Upon demand, Bango released me out of his tight grip and nodded his head before saying, "Taea, baby, I love you. Please, don't go fucking with X. Leave that to me. We have two beautiful children that need both of their parents, especially their mother."

Knowing what he said was true, I didn't acknowledge him as I fled out of the house. I didn't care to hear anything about someone being out of my league. There wasn't anyone that couldn't be blessed with a Smith and Wesson. I was determined to keep Bango and myself alive for our children; I wasn't going to have it any other way. Our children meant the world to me. They were beautiful and so intelligent at a year old. Markell and Martaea were twins and the spitting image of Bango and me. Their skin tone was that of creamy caramel; they had bushy, black eyebrows like their father and big, hazel-greenish eyes courtesy of Bango. Martaea was the oldest by five minutes, and she was very bossy and loud, while Markell was submissive and quiet.

As I jumped in the front seat of Bango's black Dodge Ram truck, I had intentions of riding around to clear my mind. All of that changed soon as I left Braisedlawn, the quiet community that my grandmother, Sue, and Grandma Toot lived in. Thoughts of my wedding day flooded my head, and I aimed for the one place that I overheard Bango saying that X was at the most—Prattville.

I didn't have a strategic plan, and I knew that was one thing that I needed in order to pull the shit off. With the intentions to do something that my husband couldn't, I felt that I would be sitting on top of the world with that vicious bitch out of the way. As I approached a red light on Mobile Highway in front of Church's, there was a group of men in two white Tahoes standing behind it—in the middle of the road and in broad daylight. I recognized them immediately and rolled down my window; without a doubt, I knew that my husband called them. While I was rolling down my window, two of them walked toward the truck.

"What's up?" I asked, curiously.

"Get out of the truck and someone will take you wherever you want go," Snoogi, one of Bango's security detail, informed me.

Laughing, I had to shake my head at the foolishness. Only Bango would setup a road block so that I couldn't do anything. Not in the mood to argue with Snoogi since I knew that I wasn't going to win,

I hopped out of the front seat and strolled toward the SUV. Cursing and thanking Bango at the same time, I let him think that he was going to win this battle. I was determined to finalize shit. Somehow, I was going to find a way to the bitch that tried to destroy my world.

Chapter Ten

Bango

Since I was shot at my wedding, nothing was the same. I was constantly watching my back, barely sleeping, and bouncing from city to city to avoid the one person that damn near destroyed my wife and me. My father put a heavy security detail on me, my wife, and children. A nigga could barely shit in peace with all that detail. I kept telling my dad that it wasn't necessary, but he wasn't hearing that shit.

I never witnessed the gangster side of Reggio Esposito, and it was downright mind blowing how much power he possessed. I never knew what his position was with the northern Italian mafia, thanks to my dad's father. My paternal grandfather didn't like blacks, which caused me to be cast out. He never knew about me; if he did, I would be dead and so would my mother. My father had to keep me hidden from his dad and cease the relationship with my mother, which caused her to cease wanting to be a mother to me. My grandmother, Toot, took me into her loving arms when I was born, and my mother went on about her business. Even though my dad kept me hidden, he made sure to come and see me every other weekend, send money, setup a trust fund account, and make sure that Grandma Toot and I were straight. He never missed a birthday, the birds and bees talk, summer vacations, spring break, and other holidays. He was very in tune with my upbringing. He really hated when Grandma Toot told him that my fifteen-year-old ass was selling drugs. After that particular phone call, that nigga was in Alabama the next hour, grilling me the fuck out. Against his wishes, I continued doing what I wanted—all because I wanted to be in the presence of the most gorgeous female in the world X!

"One more head and then we can chop it up, Bango," Cobra stated in his deep, husky voice.

"A'ight," I told him as I gathered my thoughts.

M'Kai 'Cobra' James and I were not homeboys. We knew of each other because I took one of his bitches, Calundra Thompson, when we were younger. I knew that nigga loved the hell out of that chick, but I didn't give two fucks. All I saw in her was a wonderful fuck session, and sure enough, she gave me just that!

I had to pull up on Cobra while he was at his barbershop, because I received word that he was one of two guys that were delivering money to Taea since I was classified as dead. I wanted to know who was behind sending him to deliver money to my wife; a part of me knew it was X, but I had to know why. Shit wasn't adding up to me. Before I killed her, I had to know why she was sending money to my wife. Ten minutes later, Cobra turned on the closed sign and took a seat beside me.

Firing up a cigarette, he said, "What's up?"

"Who got you delivering money to my wife?" I asked as I stared into his black face.

"I'm not about to get into that. I'm just the delivery guy. Truth be told, you already know who got me delivering that money," he said, blowing smoke out of his nose and mouth while looking into my eyes.

"X?"

Not responding, he just looked at me.

"Why?"

"Obviously, she's feeling some type of way about what happened. She thinks you are dead, man. The first time she handed me that brown envelope, she broke down. That was the first time I ever saw her so distraught, drunk, and in tears."

At the mention of X being in tears was unbelievable to me. I was the first person that ever saw her cry, and I was the first person that saw her show emotion; that statement let me knew that they had a long conversation, and I pressed him for answers.

"Y'all had a long conversation?"

"Yep, because shit didn't sit well with me. I wanted to know why in the hell she was so distraught after shooting you and then setting it in stone by calling your name," he said casually after inhaling his cigarette and then continued, "She kept saying that she didn't mean to and that Reggio was the target. She never said why he was the target, but she was hella bent on informing me that she never meant to 'kill' you. According to her, her knees buckled at the time she accidently squeezed the trigger. She also stated that once she realized that she shot you instead of Reggio, she had to make it seem like it was you she was after. She didn't want people to know that she made a mistake. That damn pride a mutherfucker!"

Taking in everything that Cobra was saying, I sat back and exhaled heavily. I had a quick decision to make since I just sent my boys to go after and kill her or it would be my wife's life that was going to be on my hands. Quickly snatching my phone off the holster, I pressed and held down on the number four button.

Seconds later, Snoogi answered in his slurred tone, "Hello."

"The hit is off. Do not fuck with X! Do not fuck with her," I made sure to say it slowly so that he could hear me.

"We can't fuck with her anyways... that bitch popped out of the window with a sawed off and laid it down. The truck slammed into a tree. The Yukon is laid on its side on fucking fire," he said in a pissed off tone. I tried to hold in my laughter, because that crazy heifer was still on it.

"Okay, make sure if y'all see her do not touch her. Understood?"

"Yeah," he replied curtly before hanging up the phone.

Placing my phone back on the holster, I looked at Cobra and I couldn't produce anything to say other than, "I'm sorry for taking Calundra from you."

He laughed so hard and said, "Mane, I'm glad you did take her. I would've never met Serenity and married her."

"Yo' doggish ass settled down?" I asked in a shocked tone before chuckling.

"You are a fine one to talk about doggish, nigga," he chuckled while I was still laughing.

"True. True."

"All jokes aside, I really think X was in love with you. You know that uncle of hers wasn't wrapped to tight in the head."

"No, he wasn't. What happened to him anyways?"

"I guess X got tired of his ass. He did her so wrong, man."

Now, that statement truly had me confused as fuck. She was the boss of all bosses, and I had to know how in the hell did Tyke do her wrong.

"Why you say that?" I inquired curiously.

"From the conversation that she and I had, she told me that Tyke made sure that she was never happy—love wise. He was hella bent on her not having a personal life. She went into full detail about you and her. I studied her to see if she was lying and she wasn't. She was a different person while we were talking about such an important portion of her life—you. After she got pregnant by you,

Tyke made her have an abortion and told her that if she ever showed or expressed being in love or loving someone else again, he would kill her."

"Wait, pregnant?" I said loudly as I almost fell out of the chair I was sitting in.

"By your response, I'm assuming you didn't know."

"No," I stated, jaws clenching and unclenching.

I grew completely quiet as I thought about when I could've gotten her pregnant, and it dawned on me when.

Shaking my head, I spat nastily, "That's why she got real nasty with me and disappeared for two months back in '06."

With that thought, I dapped up Cobra and told him thank you followed by take it easy.

Once I was secured in the front seat of the black Escalade my father told me to ride around in, I was a ball of confusion, frustration, and anger. I didn't know who to be pissed at the most, X or Tyke. With another issue on my hands, I was, more than ever, ready to get my hands on her ass. I wanted some fucking answers, and I needed them.

***

It was 11:00 p.m., and the house was completely quiet minus the humming from the refrigerator when I decided to walk into my grandmother's backyard with a blunt, two cigarettes, and my cell phone. It was cold outside, yet I was hot as hell from the conversation that Cobra and I had earlier. Firing up my blunt and hitting it three times caused my mind to go on a whirlwind. I began thinking about the times I was alone with X and began to fall in love with her.

I remembered how my heart used to flutter when she flashed that beautiful smile with the train tracks on her top teeth. I remembered the way she tasted and arched her back when she was having an orgasm. I remembered the first time she told me that she loved me after I told her that several times without a response. Our conversations were beautiful, quality time was splendid, and sexing was amazing. All of that changed because Tyke was an asshole. He was the reason why X and I never went any further than what we did. He scared the living shit out of her, and for that, I would never forgive him!

X was a bad ass, true enough, and I admired that in her. However, at the end of the day, she was intelligent, gorgeous, and thoughtful person. The only way X turned into a beast was when she was threatened; other than that, she was the person that everyone went to so that they could feed their families. They knew she broke bread with her men; they knew she would look out for them. They knew that she wouldn't cheat anyone out of their money. X'Zeryka Nicole Toole was all about her teaming winning and loyalty.

Tired of thinking about her, I decided to call her. With the soft strokes of my hand touching my cold phone, her line was ringing.

On the third ring, her soft, beautiful voice graced the line with a simple "Hello."

"X," I said as I inhaled my blunt.

"Yes," she asked in a shaken tone.

"Can you meet me in thirty minutes anywhere of your choosing?"

There was a long pause in the phone as I heard her shuffling away from something, followed by the soft closure of what could've been a door.

"I never meant to hurt you. My angle was your father. Never in a million years, would I have hurt you, Marcus," she said softly before sniffling followed by light sobs.

"Can you meet me?" I asked sternly and urgently.

"I'm not in close range, Marcus."

"I don't give a fuck. I need to see you face to face, and I need to ask these questions while I'm in your face. X, you owe me. I received information from Cobra today, and it's been sitting on my brain all day... I want a one on one talk with you."

"Okay, and where?" she finally stated in a low tone.

"You name the place, and I'll be there."

"Our old spot in Clanton," she said as I heard a door open in the background followed by keys lightly jiggling.

"Okay. I'm leaving Montgomery now."

"K," she announced before hanging up the phone.

Tossing the little piece of the blunt on the ground, I hopped off the swing and jogged back into the house. Halfway down the hallway, I saw a silhouette of Taea. Her little sneaky ass was trying to get some information; I hoped like hell she didn't hear my conversation with X.

"Why are you out of bed?" I asked into the darkness.

"Because your body was missing from the bed, and I wanted to check on the kids," she whispered.

Before I walked into my old childhood room, I stopped by the room my babies were occupying. As I approached their toddler bed, I planted two kisses on their foreheads and told them that daddy loves them. Once I was done loving on my sleeping children, I headed to the room Taea and I were occupying. Taking a seat on the bed, my wife just stared at me as I put on my Timbs and slid my hoodie over my head.

"Where are you going?" she asked softly.

"To handle some business," I told her as I turned around to walk toward her.

"I want to come."

"No. Your place is right here with our children. It's late... get some rest. I promise you, I will be back by your side before the sun rises," I replied against the crook of her neck after I kissed it.

"Okay," she replied defenselessly.

Giving her a long and passionate kiss, I exited my grandmother's home and jumped in the passenger seat of my father's issued SUV. Clanton was not far from Montgomery, but it wasn't close either. Given my history of fast driving, I would be there in forty-five minutes.

Along the way, I thought about what X's answers were going to be. I thought about how she would react to seeing me in the flesh. A smile crept across my face as I imagined that she would flash that beautiful smile as tears slid down her face. I knew that I was supposed to have been dead as mad with her, but from Cobra's testimony, I knew that I had to let the two-sided decision go.

All I wanted was answers to my questions, and then I could get my wife and children out of Alabama. There was a lot of hurt in the state for Taea, and I refused to have her here knowing it almost drained the life out of her.

The ride to Clanton was peaceful as there weren't any cars I had to blow my horn at or curse out. I had road rage, and I really thanked the Man above for not having many eighteen-wheelers on the road. Every six miles or so, I saw a car either jumping off an exit or climbing up one.

Upon approaching Clanton's exit, I grew antsy as I made a right turn and slid down the road. Two miles down the road, I made a left turn and was greeted with a black iron fence with the keypad in the middle of the gate. Dialing X's number, she picked up on the first ring.

"I'm here. Open the gate."

"I'm not there yet. I'm coming from Birmingham. The code is your birthday," she replied in a calm tone.

"You never changed it?" I chuckled, opening the driver's door and walking toward the gate.

"No," she laughed briefly and then stopped.

"How long will it be before you get here?" I asked, once the gate opened.

"About fifty minutes or so. I have the hazard lights on as I'm doing a hundred and ten."

"Okay. Be careful," I said before I knew it.

"Always," she said before hanging up the phone.

Hopping back in the front seat, I drove inside of the gates. In plain sight was the simple, ducked off two-bedroom manufactured home that sat at least a half of mile away from a man-made lake. Cruising to the front of the trailer, I sat in the car and smoke my cigarette. Letting my thoughts take me to a place they shouldn't have gone.

Ring. Ring. Ring.

Glancing down at my phone, it was my dad calling. I knew I had to answer it.

"Hello."

"You fucking telling me that you had a clear chance to kill that bitch and you didn't, Marcus?" he shouted in the phone. The only person that could've told him that was Taea, and I was pissed that she did that.

"Dad, not right now."

"The bitch shot you at your motherfucking wedding. She damn near killed you, and you didn't shoot that bitch's head off!"

"Dad, chill out. I know what I am doing. You don't need to be so worried about me," I told him as I put out my cigarette and fired up an already rolled blunt.

"Listen to yourself. She already had you placed in the hospital up in Birmingham months before she shot up your damn wedding."

"Dad, you don't have to tell me about the shootings that took place. I was there, remember? I haven't forgotten a thing."

"I tell you this thing here," he said strongly in his northern Italian accent and then continued, "Soon as I catch that bitch, I'mma put a bullet in her head!"

"Dad, I can handle my own. Now, please leave from down here. All you are doing is making things worse for me."

Without so much as a response, my father hung the phone up in my face, and I surely didn't lose any sleep over it. After shaking my head at the issue, I resumed my thoughts of the one woman that caused me the most issues.

At 1:15 a.m., the headlights from a car beamed through the iron gates. Not knowing if there was a surprise waiting in that car or not, I pulled out a super soaker and cocked it back. The silver Honda Accord sped rapidly toward the manufactured home, and I didn't budge until the engine and lights of the car were cut off, and X stepped out with nothing in her hands.

I slowly stepped out of the car, and I'll be damned if she didn't start running toward me. The shit caught me off guard and all I could do was open my arms up and pick her up once she was in arms reach.

"You supposed to be dead, lil' bitch," I told her as I gave her a tight hug, inhaling her sweet tantalizing scent.

Climbing down off my body, she nodded her head as she was looking down at the ground.

Lifting her head up, I said, "We need to talk about everything, starting with you disappearing in '06."

Quickly picking up her head, I saw her big eyes become teary. She nodded her head and told me to follow her.

As I was walking behind her, I kept singing in my head, *You are married. Keep your dick at bay. Get some closure. Tell her what you need and then leave. You took vows, nigga. What was once between the two of y'all ain't no damn more.*

Once inside of the cozy trailer, I saw that there were a few new furniture pieces added. As we sat comfortably on the ivory leather short sofa, I did the one thing that I shouldn't have—tongue kissed the bitch that shot me at my motherfucking wedding.

X

The entire drive to Clanton, I was on pins and needles. I didn't know what Bango was going to say or do; however, I knew that I had to get the truth off my chest. I was not expecting for him to still be so damn sexy; I was not expecting for him to stick his tongue in my mouth. I was not expecting any of his positive energy. Not understanding him, I had to push my body away from him. Standing up and clearing my throat at the same time, I played with the ends of my black t-shirt.

"You are acting like you did when I took your virginity, X," he chuckled lightly as he got up off the sofa and glared at me.

"Yeaaah," I stammered and then continued, "I'm nervous."

"X, we have done everything under the sun and moon, yet you are nervous. Why?" he said as he slowly started walking toward me, licking his juicy lips.

"I've always been nervous around you. I just knew how to mask it. Now, I can't mask it."

Nodding his head, he replied, "Did you ever love me?"

That question threw me for a loop. I didn't know how to interpret the question, but I did answer it by nodding my head.

"What was the reason why you left for two months back in the summer of '06?"

Dropping my head to the ground and not able to produce any words, I started playing with my fingers until he raised his voice and demanded that I answer him.

"Tyke found out that I was pregnant, made me have an abortion, and exiled me to the worst part of Africa as my punishment."

"What the fuck? You were just a teenager, X," Bango said loudly, clearly angry.

Not saying anything I retreated back to the short, ivory sofa. My mind traveled back to the day that Tyke told never to get exclusively involved with anyone else, or he would kill me. The tears flooded my face and the floodgates opened. Only Tyke knew how to make me cry and make me feel like I wished I was never born.

"X, don't do that... please don't do that," Bango announced softly as he took a seat next to me and rubbed my knee gently.

"I'm tired of this shit, Bango. Tyke is dead, and he still has a hold on me. I wanted this street shit, I really did, but not to have love is a motherfucker. I deserve to have money and be loved at the same time. I've done some horrible shit to you, and all I can do is pray that you forgive me," I sobbed as I held my head down, ashamed to look him in the face.

"I just forgave you when I talked to Cobra, yesterday."

With a sigh of relief, there were still things in the air that needed to be discussed, and he had to hear me out.

Wiping the tears away, I softly called his name, "Bango?"

"Yeah?"

"Your father must die. I know that is harsh, but hear me out," I quickly stated, seeing that he was ready to dispute my actions.

"You know you gotta explain that one," he stated as he leaned back on the sofa and gave me his full attention.

"Remember when we were eighteen and we were up in the A at The W?"

"Yep."

"Those guys that were after us were sent by your father because of Tyke. I don't know what my uncle told your father, but he's out to kill me. That is unacceptable in my eyes."

Taking a moment of silence, Bango sat with a quizzical look on his face before he said anything. I took that time to explain everything that I knew and how I got the information. Hopping off the sofa, Bango shook his medium-sized head and blew air out of his mouth.

"That's my father, yo!" he shouted as he looked at me with a worried expression spread across his face.

Not saying anything but ensuring to move slowly, I reached into the back of my loose sweatpants and placed my Glock on the table. Slouching down on the sofa, I had some questions of my own.

"Did you ever love me?"

"Yes," he replied without breaking eye contact or even hesitating to answer.

"Why?"

"Because you were a cool ass person outside of being the bossy bitch that you are. You handled business well, and made sure to look out for me. You and I have a lot of things in common. We bonded over having sucky ass mothers. You are very selfless when it came down to helping people. You really ain't a bad person, X... you just can't be trusted when you get pissed off."

"You know that I didn't have Rodrigo rape Taea, right?"

Rodrigo was a no nonsense, flashy street runner of mine. He and others sold small quantities of my quality dope throughout the city of Montgomery.

"Speaking of that, explain, now."

"He was only supposed to have scared her. I gave him strict instructions on not touching a hair on her head. I didn't want you to leave the game. I liked being in your presence. I couldn't physically have you, but I loved the little conversations that we did have. I loved the little sexual escapades we had from time to time, and I didn't want to give that up."

"Do you think Tyke could've gotten in Rodrigo's ear?" he probed as he walked to the kitchen and pulled out two short, crystal glasses.

"Yes."

"Now, I have a question of my own... were you excited when you found out that I had gotten you pregnant?" he asked as he filled the first cup full with bourbon and was about to fill the next when I told him fill my cup with juice.

Looking at me, he replied after laughing, "Juice? So, you are fucking saint now? Just the other day you were in Miami sucking down tequila."

Nodding my head and lightly laughing, I responded, "I surely was but I'm done drinking for a while, and to answer your question, yes, I was excited to be carrying your seed but at the same time, I was scared as shit."

No more talking took place until he poured apple juice in a glass and brought the cups to the front room. As he handed me the glass, I made sure to touch his hands. I sighed heavily as I felt the soft hands that caressed my body more times than I could count. The same hands that held me when I had those fucked up dreams. Those hands that made my inner body sing higher notes than Aretha Franklin.

"X, I can't have my father dead. I just won't go for it. We gotta come up with a solution."

"He's at me hard, and it has nothing to do with me shooting you. Hell, I came to your wedding to off his ass. I didn't want anyone to know that I made a mistake and shot you. I know it's stupid of me not to show that I made a mistake, but I had a reputation to uphold. I'm truly sorry for what I did. I never forgave myself for what happened to you."

"I know."

Shocked at his response, I had to know how he knew that I never had forgiven myself; therefore, I asked.

"How you know?" I asked as I sipped from the crystal glass, all the while looking at him.

"I been underneath your nose for a quite some time, X. You went into 'hiding'... not because of you were afraid of retaliation, but because you were mourning me. Within the third month of recovery, I posted up in the back of your safe house and watched you cry and beat yourself up. I had my rifle ready to knock you off, but soon as you screamed my name in pure pain... I knew something was wrong. There was no way in hell that you would show that type of emotion for someone that you meant to kill. You still cry about me. You've been sending my wife money, and to this day she doesn't know that Kutta isn't the one sending money."

"I taught you a lot about how to move in silence, huh?" was the only thing that I could say because he really had plenty of opportunities to knock me off the map. I was real vulnerable after I thought he was dead. Bango was more than a worker and a part-time lover to me; he was damn near my other half. I learned so much from him that I couldn't bare not seeing him monthly or at least make quality dope for him to distribute.

"Yes, you have and if I never paid attention to the number one thing you taught me... you would've been a dead ass. I had a clear chance to shoot you at Chivalry, and do you know Taea is pissed off at that?"

The number one thing I taught him was to pay attention to body language. The language of a person's body would tell you anything you wanted to know, regardless if they were lying or not.

"I'm quite sure she is. How do I make things right with us? Not on the level that we were once on but a gucci level. I'm ready to leave the game once I get your father out of my hair," I replied with my head low.

"We already okay. You don't have to worry about me. I forgive you, but now I need to ask you to forgive me," he sighed heavily before grabbing my hand.

Not understanding why he would ask me to forgive him when he did nothing to me, I stared at him with a weird look on my face.

"You haven't done anything to me, so why are you asking for my forgiveness?" I inquired, giving him my full attention.

"One, I didn't have your back like I said that I always would. Two, I killed your grandmother," he announced in a disappointed tone.

I felt the wind being knocked out of me as I dropped the crystal glass on the floor. The small hairs on the nape of my neck rose, and I felt my chest closing in. My breathing became erratic, which caused my eyes to briefly land on my gun. Not being able to think clearly, I slowly got up off the sofa and walked in the kitchen and took a seat at the kitchen table.

"Whyyy?" I sobbed, not looking at him.

"Tyke wanted someone to shoot up the house, and Big Shawn got me to do it as part of being initiated into his lil' organization."

Not able to take hearing that my grandmother was slaughtered because of Tyke, I hopped up from the kitchen table—it was clearly time for me to go. I didn't want to say anything else to Bango or look him in the face. I had sworn that when I found out who was in charge of ordering that hit and following through with it, I would kill all that were involved. At that moment of hearing Bango say that he was the one that did it and given our prior history, I gave everything up to the Man above to handle.

Snatching up my gun and placing it in the back of my sweatpants, I told Bango, "All is forgiven. You have a great life."

"X'Zeryka, I wante—"

"I don't want to hear any of that shit. What's done is done! I forgive you, okay. I told my truths, you told yours, and now we can go on about our business without retaliation," I stated angrily and then continued, "I'm going to kill your father. He will not cease my life and that of my unborn child because of some shit that Tyke said to him."

"Unborn child?" he asked quizzically.

"Yeah. Now, come on so that I can lock this place up and go get some sleep."

"Tony's?"

"Nope."

"Whose?" he asked with an attitude. I looked at Bango like he lost his damn mind. There was no need in him getting an attitude about me being pregnant. He was fucking married.

"That's none of your business," I spat nastily, clearly irritated by him questioning me.

"You are right... I apologize," he said as he hopped up from the sofa and started strolling to the front door.

Mind all over the place, I didn't hear anything that he said until he shoved me against the wall and stared in my face before placing his face close to mine.

"Did you hear me?" he stated sternly in my face.

"No."

"Who baby is you pregnant with?"

"Rondon's."

He began to flinch his jaws, but kept his mouth closed. I wanted to inquire what got his boxers in a bunch, but he didn't mind expressing why he was so upset.

"You fucking that nigga? Out of all niggas, you are fucking Rondon...your fucking goon? That is the number one rule, you don't fuck the help," he spat slowly, walking backwards to look at me.

"You were my help, and we fucked numerous times, so tell me a better reason you are pissed, Marcus," I retorted with a smirk on my face.

"Nothing, man. All is forgiven. Have a nice life," he yelled as he strolled past me with an angry look on his face.

"Same to you."

I couldn't move because I surely didn't know what the hell just happened in my face. Things were not adding up. I didn't have the slightest clue why Bango was so pissed at me for getting knocked up by Rondon when he had a whole wife and two beautiful children attached to him.

In a complete daze from the one part of conversation that kept coming to the forefront of my brain, I slid onto the ground and wept. I didn't know how I was going to get over the revelation that Bango shot up my grandmother's house and flatlined her in September of '04. I was one hurt individual but nothing hurt more than the conversation that I had with Keithia once I answered her call.

"Hello," I said weakly as I stared at the floor and images of me holding my grandmother's lifeless body.

"Tony's body has been found," she said in a sad tone.

"Nooooo, Keithia don't tell me that... don't you fucking dare tell me no shit like that," I cried out, sobbing even louder at the same time Bango ran back inside of the trailer.

My whole heart was hurting, and I couldn't understand how he was dead when I ordered Ruger to release him. I didn't want him to die; that's why I didn't kill him to begin with.

"No, I'm not lying. Marsha and Landon went to view his body a couple of hours ago. A group of people on County Road One saw a body lying on the ground, in front of a stop sign and called the police."

County Road One, that is not far from my safe house. God, please don't let Ruger have killed Tony because it will be hell to pay, I thought as I continued to cry and pray for Tony's children.

"What's wrong, X?" Bango asked as he rubbed my back, gently.

Ignoring Bango, I had to know how Tony died.

"How did he die, Keithia?"

"Shot in the front and back of his head."

When she told me that, the phone slipped out of my hands and landed on the floor. I was hollering. There was no way in hell he was supposed to have been shot. I gave Ruger clear instructions on what I wanted done. It was clear that he didn't respect my wishes, and it was clear that he thought he ran the show; therefore, I had to show him and the others remaining that until I finished all of my deeds, I ran the motherfucking show! I had a wonderful plan for Ruger's ass, and he better be motherfucking ready because it was officially war, and no one could deliver war the way that I could!

Before I picked the phone up off the ground, I hung up in Keithia's face and placed a call to J-Money. On the third ring, he answered sleepily, "What up, Chief?"

"Go snatch Big Shawn up and take him to The House of Pain, call Ruger and Rondon... tell them to get their motherfucking asses there!" I yelled angrily as my emotions flooded through me.

"Yes, ma'am, Chief," he said obediently.

After I hung up the phone, Bango looked at me worriedly and then said, "Talk to me."

"I'm done talking... back to that X I go. Don't get in my way... this time it won't be a fucking mistake," I spat nastily as I got my ass up off the floor.

Halfway up off the floor, I was slammed on the ground with Bango on top of me. He had an ugly look on his face and spoke clearly, "Don't you ever threaten me again, or I will kill you... don't fucking make me!"

"Fuck you! I hate you!" I spat as I glared at him.

Slowly getting up off me, Bango replied, "No you don't because you love me just like I love you."

"Go home to your wife. I got business to handle," I replied as he bent down and picked me up.

Sighing heavily, he asked a question that I wished he had not, "May I taste you for the last time?"

"Go home to your wife!" I spat as tears welled in my eyes while feeling a tingling sensation between my legs.

Walking toward the sofa, Bango put me down gently and then responded, "You feeling that fuck nigga, Rondon, aren't you? Any other time, you would've jumped on me."

"Go home to your wife. I do a lot of things, but fucking around with a married man is not one of them!"

"Whatever, man," he replied as he looked at me nastily and walked toward the door and then continued nastily, "I should have my wife terminate that pregnancy."

That shit set me the fuck off, and I'll be damned if we didn't tear up the manufactured home. Who was he to tell me some shit like that? Who was he to be all in his damn feelings when he clearly didn't fight for our love? Who in the fuck he had me mistaken with? Pregnant or not, I showed my entire ass—right up to the point when I was on the floor with my shirt ripped off me, lying on the plush black carpet with an angry Bango standing on top of me as I stared at the barrel of his gun to my face, those scary feelings that I had back in 2003 appeared, causing me to drift back to the one day that really put me on the map of being a vicious Queenpin.

Chapter Twelve

X

May 2003

"X, this here is a nick," my uncle, Tyke, spoke calmly as he pointed his black, long but chunky forefinger toward a flaky, sparkly, yellow-greyish, small rock-like thing.

As he went down the nicely polished rectangle, dark maple table, pointing at different sizes of straight drop dope, I was mesmerized by the texture and hue. I was an eager thirteen-year-old girl, learning my uncle's trade— selling and manufacturing of the powerful drug. I was excited that I was learning another trade, but I was tired of being schooled on this particular one. That's all my uncle talked about for the past six months; I knew he was grooming me to take over his organization one day, and I knew without a doubt that I was going to do just that.

After four hours of him schooling me on the different sizes, the prices of each, and showing me how to be a great cook and distributor of quality dope, I was able to get ready for dance class. I have been in dance classes since I was in preschool. I loved everything about dance; the swaying of the body, and the complete quietness when you are in tune with your body, mind, and soul. Plus, dancing was a great way to exercise.

When we arrived at Cloudia's Dance House, I was relieved to see my dance mates. Before I left Tyke's presence, I kissed him on the cheek, told him that I loved him, and hopped out of his freshly cleaned blue-black Lexus. As I made it to the entrance door, I waved goodbye to my uncle before he drove off, heading to safe house ten, which was one of the eleven cook houses.

"Okay, young ladies, let's switch things up a bit. We are going to do a little hip-hop dancing with a little rump shaking," Ms. Cloudia spoke loudly.

Ms. Cloudia was in her mid-twenties. She possessed the body of a supermodel. Her skin color was that of a Hershey bar. She had big, brown eyes that were surrounded with black eyelashes that were perfectly curled. She had a crooked tooth that stood out, but it made her smile more unique. The sound of Lil Jon's voice blared through the speakers, and I broke out into a smooth dance of twerking. I whirled and twirled my body as if I were at home standing in front of my mirror.

"Yes, yes, ladies, copy exactly what X'Zeryka is doing. This is the art of hip-hop with a little rump shaking," Ms. Cloudia exclaimed as she shook her booty. The entire dance session was nothing but dancing like the women did on BET's Uncut videos. Truly enjoying today's session, I didn't want it to end. Therefore, I was already wishing for next Monday to arrive so that I could be amongst my dance mates and Ms. Cloudia.

Looking at the time on the clock, it read three-thirty; the time came for us to leave, and I was somewhat disappointed. Quickly gathering my belongings and placing my white Oasis on my feet, I tied my shoes and began to walk out the door when my gal pal, Julia, called my name.

"X'Zeryka!" Julia squealed.

I turned around to see her slender, pale, freckled face walking as if her feet were hurting.

"What's up?" I questioned with a bright smile upon my face.

"Why are you so happy, girl?"

"You know I'm always a happy girl," I giggled.

"What are you doing this summer?"

"I have no idea what my grandmother and uncle are planning for the summer. I know it involves Florida, as usual," I voiced in a high-pitched tone.

Since I can remember, Florida has always been our destination during the summer time.

"Ask your grandmother and uncle if I can tag along. Pretty please," she begged as she placed her hands together and tucked them comfortably under her chin.

"Okay," I lied through my pretty white, train-tracked teeth.

There was no way in hell I was going to ask them if Julia could tag along. This summer was going to be all about me. I was on the rise of being the most beautiful, intelligent, young female to conquer the baddest, well-established distributor in Miami. All that training that Tyke put me through was because he wanted me to reel in the one motherfucker that he couldn't—Francesco Augello. Tyke didn't think I knew that, but I mastered the skill of eavesdropping.

As I was about to continue conversing with Julia, I heard my grandmother calling my name angrily. *Oh shit, what have I done?* I asked myself as I thought back on things that I could've done.

"Ma'am!" I stated while turning around to meet my gorgeous, yet semi-angry grandmother.

"Let's go," she stated firmly with her hands on her hips.

Immediately nervous by her tall, strong posture and tone, I refused to show that I was nervous and scared. Looking at Julia, I told her that I would call her later on. As I said goodbye to my instructor and dance mates, I wondered what in the fuck I did. I was an A-honor roll student, didn't get into trouble, and my room was clean.

The entire time to my grandmother's 1999 white Buick LeSabre, my mind was on go mode. For the life of me, I couldn't understand why she was upset with me. Upon me closing the passenger door, my heart beat rapidly because I knew she was getting ready to unleash the dragon on me for God knows what.

"How was your weekend with your uncle?" she voiced casually as she started the engine on her car.

"It was great. His new girlfriend took us shopping, out to eat, and to the new arcade," I boasted proudly. I couldn't wait to strut around junior high in the latest outfits that my uncle purchased. There were some females that weren't too keen of me because I stayed in my own lane, and I considered myself as worthy of not being in their presence.

"I know that your uncle gives you money for making A's, but X'Zeryka Nicole Toole where did you get two thousand dollars from?" my grandmother asked as she held up the wad of cash that I had stashed in my money jar, which was in the back of my closet. There wasn't any need in getting upset about her snooping around my things. If I told the semi-truth, then the discussion will be over with, like I've always done.

"That's the money I have saved over the course of three years from my report cards, babysitting, tutoring, washing Tyke and 'nem cars, doing clerical work for the church, and chore money," I stated as I fumbled with my hands, all the while staring into my grandmother eyes.

Keep looking into her eyes. Keep your eyes still and innocent looking. She will never know the real truth about some of your earnings if you continue with the good girl role, I said to myself repeatedly until she put the gearshift in drive.

"Oh-kay. I'm so proud of you for saving your money. What are you saving for?"

"A car, college tuition, and other expenses like ball dances, and etc."

Who said you are getting a car?" she questioned quizzically.

"You did," I laughed. I was glad that the conversation about the two thousand dollars I had accrued was not up for discussion anymore. I really hated lying to the one woman who loved me unconditionally.

We continued with general conversation until we pulled into our three-bedroom, two bath, white and green suburban home in the inner city of Prattville. Once in the house, I completed my usual routine of taking a shower, putting my clothes in the dirty hamper, and enjoying my time with my grandmother, until it was time for bed.

After the ten o'clock news, my grandmother waltzed into my room, kissed me on the forehead, and told me goodnight. Showing her the same type of love, I faked a yawn. Once she left my room, I turned off my light, got under the covers, and stared throughout my dark room, waiting for the perfect time to complete my mission.

An hour later, I was in my closet with a flashlight looking for the box with my prized possession. As I placed my hands on the small, purple and pink flowered jewelry box, a wide smile crept across my face. I lifted the top and removed the inside shelf to view the precious bagged fish-scale like contents; a note lay under the bag. I rushed to open and read what it had to say: X, the ball is in your court now. Make your uncle proud. In the top of your closet is a prepaid phone. Turn it on; you should have a sale coming around midnight. Make sure to keep it on silent and out of Ma's way. DO NOT LET HER FIND ANY OF THIS. TAKE EXTRA CARE OF BOTH ITEMS.

As I read the note over and over again, I became nervous. After I gathered my thoughts and glanced at the time, I hurriedly put on all-black clothing, retrieved the cellular device, the bagged items, and my Cross, .22 Special. I stuck them in different pockets of my black jeans. Knowing that I had everything on me, I sat patiently until it was time for me to catch a sale. Sitting on the edge of my bed ready for the cell phone to go off, I was excited about serving a junkie.

Exactly at midnight, a long vibration came from the prepaid flip phone. Opening the text, it simply stated: two dubs MP. MP stood for Monk Park. With the known destination and how much the individual wanted, I quickly separated two twenty dollar rocks from the rest of the bag and placed them in a bag of their own. Hopping off my bed, I aimed for my bedroom window. Upon successfully getting out of the house, I hopped on my bike and peddled like crazy as I rushed to Mont Park, which was three minutes away.

Upon arriving at the park, I didn't see a car or anyone. I became extremely nervous. I knew damn well my uncle didn't send me out here on a fluke mission. Realizing that was what my uncle did, anger rose in the pit of my stomach. Moments later, I saw a figure moving swiftly behind two trees, thirty steps ahead of me. As I kept my eyes on the figure, my phone vibrated. Quickly whipping it out, I read the message: Come up here. After reading the message, I stuffed the phone back into my back pocket and strolled my dark-green and black bike towards the tall trees.

As I approached the person standing in all-black, I had an eerie feeling. Something about the way that he stood didn't settle right with me. Even though I had that feeling, I dropped my bike to the ground and walked closer to the man. As the individual came close to me with an uneasy posture, I knew that this wasn't about a sale. Even though I was scared at what could happen, I didn't let it show. My heart was telling me to pick up my bike and get the hell away, but my mind kept replaying the hardest drill sergeant of the Marine Corps say, "Don't you move a fucking muscle, study the individual, and then take action."

With that inner thought, I stood my ground as the man came closer toward me. My right hand slowly moved toward my back and landed comfortably on my Cross.

Once the man approached me, his creepy voice chuckled, "Your uncle was smart to send your little, young ass out here."

Instantly, I began to pray and hold on tighter to my Cross. *God, please let me make it out this situation without having to shoot this nigga, I* thought heavily as I rubbed the Cross's handle.

"Call your uncle and tell him to get his motherfucking ass down here now!" the angry man yelled, inches away from my face.

"You want him so badly, you call him," I spoke softly but sternly, staring at him, knowing that I should've been shot his dumb ass. Honestly, I really didn't know what to do; I was scared as hell. The fake kills were completely easy. I guess because I knew the target wasn't living.

"Oh, you ain't gonna call him?" the man stated as he quickly jacked me up by the collar of my black shirt and slammed me on the ground.

Soon as my body touched the rocky hard surface, I was wildly swinging my arms. Some of my punches were connecting and others didn't. Trying to get him away from me, I wasn't successful. Squatting over my abdominal region with my wrists in a tight hold in his right hand, the man looked at me and said nastily, "Everything on you, I'm finna take it... lil' bitch."

As he was running his hands across my front pockets, I asked with a shaky voice, "What the fuck you doing?"

Not replying to me, I began to vigorously rock my body from side to side, so that he wouldn't get the precious contents that were tucked in my pockets. Determined to grab ahold of the situation, I had to figure out some type of way to get the man's face close to mine so that I could head butt his stupid ass. The only thing I knew to do was wiggle and talk shit about Tyke killing him, which finally paid off when he raised his short, black, fat hand and brought it down with great force across the left side of my face. The sting to my cheek brought tears down. Thinking back to the last motherfucker that decided she wanted to slap me, anger coursed through my body, and I found the strength that I desperately needed to bring my head forward and connect it to his nose.

"Ahh, shit, you little bitch," he stated angrily as he grabbed his nose, briefly before I kneed him in the balls.

I was expecting the man to hop up and walk away, which would've gave me time to get my Cross out. Instead, that motherfucker went into beast mode on my stomach and chest region as I laid on the ground, barely defending myself. I clearly wasn't ready for his attack on me. As I laid on that ground praying that I would made it out of the situation, I wished that I had stayed my ass at home. Knowing that dying wasn't an option, I had to get it together.

The last blow he sent to my chest laid my ass flat out on the ground, which gave him free reign to pull out the two precious bags that held my uncut dope. Looking up at the clear, starry night, defenseless, hurting, pride and ego hurt, ashamed, and disappointed in myself, I prayed that I would find the strength to get my ass up off that ground and let that motherfucking nigga know that I wasn't to be fucked with.

"Your uncle should've sent your bitch ass to a better training camp than the one he did. You are no match for this dope world. You are laying on that ground like a helpless little bitch," the man laughed in my face as he dangled the bags he retrieved out of my pockets.

Staring into his face with sad eyes, I let the tears continue to slide down my slender cheeks, and lightly cried out, "I know, but my uncle is making me do this. I don't want this lifestyle. I'm just a young girl."

Shaking his head, the man commanded before walking away from me, "Get off that ground and go home, little girl. Tyke should be ashamed for what he got you out here doing."

Soon as that bitch turned his back and began walking away from me, I reached for my gun. With bolts of pain running through my torso region and gun in my hand, I squeezed the trigger, placing two bullets in each of his legs. As he dropped to the ground, I slowly got up. Looking around the park and then toward the street, I saw a few house lights turn on. The noise from the gun was probably the reason for their lights being on, and I was sure that someone was going to call the police. Quickly forgetting all about my pain, I was instantly in panic mode. I didn't want to go to jail, so I had to move quickly.

Walking rapidly toward the motherfucker, I cursed myself out over time for letting him overpower me. Once I was standing over the fuck nigga's body, he began to speak before I cut him off, "Please, don't kill me. I'm sorry that I attacked you. Please, please, I have children at home. I—"

"Shut the fuck up," I growled angrily as I aimed the gun at his head and continued talking in the same tone, "You made several wrong decisions tonight. One, trying to rob me. Two, putting your fucking hands on me, and three, not respecting me, bitch nigga. Fuck your kids."

My hands were shaky as I unloaded the entire clip into his head his. Far off, I heard the sirens wailing. Really in panic mode, I quickly grabbed my two bags and searched his body for any valuables. Hearing the sirens approaching, I rushed to shove the items into my pockets, put my Cross in the back of my pants, and hopped on my bike. Choosing a wooded trail versus the way I came, I flew from the scene. By the time I passed an old warehouse building, I realized that I didn't pick up the shell casings. Damn near about to cry, I sucked that shit up and rode my bike faster to the house. The three-minute ride seemed like it took forever. My upper torso was burning badly, I was scared that the police were going to find the shell casings, and most importantly, I was scared shitless that my uncle was going to be severely disappointed in me.

When I arrived home, I made sure not to make a sound. I strolled quickly to the back of the utility shed. I placed my Cross and the money that I took off my first victim in a secret box that I had buried behind the shed, in the ground.

I was glad when I climbed my sore body through my window. Immediately, I rushed to take the items out of my pockets and threw them on the bed. Peeling off my clothes and placing them in a special plastic bag that Tyke gave me, I sighed heavily before throwing the bag into the top, far right, back corner of my closet. To ensure that my grandmother didn't see it, I moved some of my useless items toward the front of the closet. Afterwards, I put my pajamas back on and slowly walked to the bathroom. As I passed the kitchen, I heard my grandmother's hardcore snore. Her snores reminded me of bears growling; that woman slept hard, and I was very thankful for that.

After leaving the bathroom, I stopped in the kitchen to take two Advil. The pain I experienced was on another level; it was worse than being on my period. Finally arriving to my resting spot, my body began to relax; however, my mind was on go mode.

Before I called it a night, I retrieved the house phone from the black nightstand beside my bed and called Tyke.

"Why are you up so late, little girl?" he questioned in a deep voice as he yawned.

"I feel like I'm about to have an anxiety attack," I stated in a low, anxious tone, hoping that he would catch on.

"Why? Because you got six little, pissy-tailed boys trying to court your young ass," he chuckled. Tyke made sure to put emphasis on the word six, and I knew right then that he knew about the six shell casings.

Wanting to know how he knew that I left them, I refrained from asking him. I felt that he was close by watching to ensure that I was safe. With that thought, I grew angry because if he was watching the entire time, then why in the fuck did he let that nigga attack me in that manner?

So, I simply replied weakly as I bit down on my bottom lip, "Yes."

Tyke's heartedly laughter interrupted my thoughts, which caused me to frown.

After he finished laughing, he replied sternly, "Well, there's a good thing your Uncle Tyke told those six boys to back the fuck up off you. This is my last time telling you that I'm not going to put up with it. You don't want to piss me off, now do you?"

"No, sir," I voiced as I felt disappointed in myself.

"Good. Now, go to bed."

"Yes, sir," I voiced before hanging up the phone.

After I got off the phone with him, I thought about my actions and shook my damn head. Before closing my eyes, I mumbled, "Next time, I won't fail. I am determined to be the best and most ruthless Queenpin this nation has seen. This morning's event has shown me that I have to go hard as a female."

My life was hellish because I chose for it to be. I didn't have to choose the path that I did. I could've been anything I wanted, yet at the age of thirteen, I was hell bent on learning the one trade that I wish I never had. That night should've taught me that the dope life wasn't all that it was cracked up to be. I should've known that my uncle didn't care about me because if he did, he would've stopped Tony's father from attacking me—which I hadn't learned until well into Tony's and my sexship.

The year of 2003 had a way of shaping me into the person I was today.

Chapter Thirteen

Juvy

When I woke up, my vision was blurry, and I had a headache out of this world. My feet and hands were tightly bound to the chair I was sloppily sitting in. Trying to remember where I was at, it quickly came back once I saw Ms. Jockton and the light-skin duo smiling wickedly at me.

"Good afternoon, Juvy," the strong Italian voice spoke from behind me, interrupting my thoughts.

With my head wobbling from side to side, I tried to turn it but the pain grew intense. Not wanting to increase the pain, I stopped trying to look the man in the face. Even though I was hurting, I wanted to know why in the hell I was tricked and held hostage. Without me having to ask, the strong voiced man answered my question.

"Nice to finally meet you, Juvy, I'm Reggio Esposito. You are a valuable asset to me right now. That is the only reason why you are still alive. I need some information... mainly on that bitch, X," the man spoke as he walked in front of me.

Not responding, I sat uncomfortably in the chair while observing the pale male's appearance. He was six foot three, somewhere around 230 pounds of pure muscle with jet black hair that was cut in that white man's hairstyle, and bushy, black eyebrows. As the man stood in front of me, he toyed with an expensive gold watch that sat comfortably on his left wrist.

Slowly holding my head up to look the man in his face, I said, "What do you want?"

"I'm so glad that you are willing to help me out. You see, that bitch, X, must die. She shot one of my sons at his wedding and shot him several times when they were in a shootout... months prior to his wedding. Her uncle told me that she wouldn't stop until my son was dead, and that she was very dangerous," the man hissed as he crouched low to look into my eyes.

Upon him mentioning *sons*, one particular thing came back to me that was mentioned in my early teen years—Bone and Fish's father was dead. Now, I was truly one confused guy. There were so many questions that I had to ask. Why did they lie about their father, and what was the reason for them lying to me? However, now wasn't the time to ask.

"I'm assuming you want to know her location?" I questioned, staring into Reggio black eyes.

Laughing hysterically while looking at the Jocktons, he replied, "You are truly a smart cookie. Of course, I want her location."

Knowing that this was the only way I was going to live so that I could murder them, it was well advised that I help him somewhat.

There was no way in hell I was going to take him straight to X's place without setting a trap for all of those sons of bitches.

"I guess I have no choice, huh?"

"Not if you want to live," he replied curtly.

"Shid, Flema ain't going to let you live once she places eyes on you anyways," Fish laughed while Bone shook his head.

Shit, she gonna go in on my ass. How in the hell am I going to get her to believe what happened to me? I thought as Fish mentioned Flema's name. I knew it was going to be some shit once I pulled up to her crib. I had to get my behind to her house asap. She needed to know that I was going to be a father to our child.

"Barius, unlock Juvy so that we can get this show on the road," Reggio commanded to Bone.

"Yes, sir," he replied while walking toward me, avoiding eye contact. That was the first time that I heard that nigga have some manners, and I did find it funny. Therefore, I laughed. As I was laughing, I wanted to knock that nigga's ass out. However, I was outnumbered and without a gun, so that thought quickly went out of the window.

"Once you have what you want, what becomes of me?" I inquired, looking at Reggio while Bone freed my legs.

Sighing heavily before sliding his hand down his strong, muscular face, he responded, "You will have to deal with my brother, Dundo. Looks like your penis has been doing some extra shit."

With a quizzical look upon my face, I had to probe further into his statement.

"Elaborate," I told him as I stood out of the chair and stretched my limbs before rubbing my ankles and wrists.

"You fucked his daughter and got her pregnant. My brother and the rest of my family isn't like me. They hate blacks, so I truly don't know what will become of you once I'm done using you," he told me bluntly.

"Who is his daughter?" I questioned quickly with a frown upon my face before finishing with another comment, "How in the hell your family don't like blacks, but you have kids by two black women?"

I had to know how does one escape a racist family, and have children with the same race that the family hates.

Turning around on his heels, he whipped out his cell phone and scrolled through it briefly. By the time he was standing inches away from me, he held the phone to my face at the same time responding to my question about his racist family, "I keep my children hidden. I take care of them, but I will not allow anyone to harm them, including family. Now, that is enough questions."

Paying more attention to the picture of the beautiful female that I smashed on several occasions with a Magnum rubber on, I cared less about his comment about his dumb ass family. Upon realizing who the broad was, I burst out in laughter. Everyone began to look at each other, because it was clear that they didn't understand why I was so damn tickled.

"What is so funny, huh, Juvy?" Reggio asked with a raised eyebrow.

"The picture you are holding up in my face... you should be holding up in Fish's and Bone's faces. They are the ones that smashed their cousin raw without a condom that night. I made sure to strap up every time I dived in her," I spat while laughing.

"Mane, what the fuck you talking about?" Bone inquired in a high-pitched timbre.

"The bitch that liked to pop Mollies and suck Jack Daniels off the dick," I chuckled while glaring into Reggio's black eyes.

"Oh shit... nawl, nawl," Bone and Fish spat in disbelief.

"Oh, yes, yes, yes," I laughed hysterically until Ms. Jockton put her two cents in.

"No need in laughing at my boys, Juvian. You are in a worse situation than they are, truth be told. You, X, and her goons are the last ones left that knows about the Jundo Village. Therefore, I would tread lightly if you want your pathetic life."

Chuckling lightly and ready to be petty with her ass, I politely said, "How does it feel to have your sons grow up without a father while he is and was fully involved in Bango's life from the time he was born? How does it feel to be kept a secret Ms. Jockton?"

I had no idea whether Reggio was heavily involved with Bango or not, but the look upon her face confirmed that I hit a nerve. Her face began to twitch, her mouth balled up, and she began to walk closer to me.

"After you help *my* sons father... you better pray that he doesn't give me the go ahead to kill you just like he did your family, lil' bastard," she spat loudly as Reggio grabbed her arm.

Anger grew in me all over again, and I gave that bitch the nastiest look while nodding my head and thinking, *I must kill your ass first, bitch!*

Ring. Ring. Ring.

Reggio looked down at his phone and quickly answered it, "Ciao."

I assumed that meant hello or some shit like that in his native language.

His face turned red as he shouted, "Che cosa!"

Once again, I didn't know what the fuck that meant, but the conversation he had on the phone had that fuck nigga going in.

Before he ended the call, Reggio spat in an agitated tone, "Bango, if you come to me with this shit again... I swear I'm going to put a hurting on your fucking back side. I don't want to hear shit else about not harming the bitch that doesn't mean you any good. Understood?"

After he ended the call with his son, Reggio looked at me and said, "Where does the bitch spend most of her time at?"

"She's a floater. She doesn't stay in too many places longer than two days," I lied, staring him straight in the face.

Ring. Ring. Ring.

Reggio phone went off again, and he was back on the angry role. However, this time he was talking in English.

"What the fuck you mean all of my men are dead? How in the hell did a cagna run through my men like that? I want her fucking head on a silver platter... do I make myself clear? Draft the best out of New Jersey," he spat angrily in the phone before hanging it up.

Enjoying the conversation, I chuckled to myself as I thought *my girl, X, and her goons showing out in 'Bama. Get them stanky motherfuckers, baby girl. I'll be up there shortly to join in on the fight.*

"I'm tired of wasting time. Everyone to their rides. Darlene, ride with me, baby," Reggio stated passionately as he held out his right hand for the light-skin duo's mother's hand. I refused to call the bitch Ms. Jockton. She was now known as the evil bitch.

On command, she sashayed her petite behind toward the man as she held a strong, 'stank' facial expression. She had the attitude of a bitch that thought she was the shit. Little did she know, she truly wasn't, and she was going to regret crossing me.

"Where are we going?" I inquired as I began to walk toward the back door of The Warehouse.

"To a spot of mine," Reggio announced rapidly.

"If I'm going to get you the information you need, I must run by my chick's house first."

"Who? Flema?" Fish joked.

Looking at him nastily while I growled, he shut the fuck up.

"Fish told Flema about the two kids that him and Tania are raising, Juvy," Bone stated while shaking his head.

Wondering why in the hell Bone was so quick to be friendly with me, I put that to the side and questioned Fish.

"Why in the fuck would you do that?" I shouted, bringing everyone to a complete stop.

"Because she tried to come for me, and I put a halt on all that shit," he spat nastily.

Shaking my head, I resumed walking out of The Warehouse at the same time Reggio was telling me not to pull any stunts. Not worrying about what the fuck he was talking about, I kept it moving toward my Hummer. The entire time I was heading to my whip, I had Flema on my mind. I didn't know what to expect when I showed my face to her. Soon as I jumped in my whip, I placed my phone on the charger and started the engine. My phone was completely dead, so there was no way for me to reach out to her.

I had some explaining to do, and I swear that I wasn't up for the questions or the vindictive shit that was going to come about. Placing the gearshift in drive, I sped out of the large, smooth parking lot of The Warehouse. By the time I touched down on Tousone Street, I powered on my phone and called Flema's phone only to be sent to the voicemail. Not caring about the third red light on Tousone Street, I pressed the hazard light button and ran that motherfucker. I didn't do the speed limit as I fled to Flema's home.

While I was driving rapidly, I thought of what to say and how to say it. I knew she was going to cry and throw shit at me, and I had to get prepared for the physical abuse she was going to render upon my body. Soon as I turned on her perfectly paved road, I saw a lot of cars in her yard. I knew then that it was about to be a bunch of shit. I was sure that she told Wilema and her mother what was told to her, which properly prompted them to tell someone else. Parking my whip on the curb in front of her house, the vibe I got from those who were standing outside wasn't a good one. With a quizzical look upon my face and a racing heartbeat, I jumped out and ambled toward the front door. People were wiping their eyes and I heard Flema's mother crying. That's when I picked up my pace and ran like hell—sliding through the front door because my balance was thrown off by the red, tan, and green welcome rug.

"Flemaaaa!" I yelled as I hopped to my feet while looking around for her.

Her family began shaking their heads as they wiped the tears away from their differently shaped faces. A chill ran through my body, and I called her name again but with more intensity, "Flema!"

"Stop calling my child's name, damn it. She's dead!" her mother spat nastily.

Soon as the word dead escaped her mouth, ran through my ears, and reached my brain, I grew weak. My knees buckled, causing me to drop to the ground as I cried for her and our unborn child's life. My soul hurt as I wept about the one person that should be cursing me out, but instead, she was dead. I couldn't take the news that was delivered to me. There was no way in hell that the last encounter that we had was on a bad note.

As tears slid down my face, I began to pray for her soul; I prayed that she forgave me for all the wrong I did and allowed to happen to her.

Not able to take any more of my prayers, I lowly murmured as the tears continued to stream down my face, "No, Flema, No! Why? I was going to do right by our child! I was!"

Chapter Fourteen

Rondon

"Have y'all talked to Chief?" I asked J-Money, Baked, and Ruger curiously.

They shook their heads with their eyebrows raised, causing me to become even more pissed off. She wasn't answering any of my calls or texts. I didn't know if she was in danger or not. I knew that I was going to lay off in her ass, soon as I placed my eyes on her. She was doing some careless shit. X was going to learn that I was nothing to play with when it came down to her being obedient, especially while pregnant.

"What are we supposed to do with Big Shawn?" Baked asked J-Money as they rolled two blunts apiece.

"I don't know but obviously, it ain't good," J-Money stated nonchalantly.

"When she called you, J-Money, how did she sound?" Ruger inquired as he fired up a Kool cigarette.

"She was on another level. I really can't explain. She was beyond pissed off... she seemed as if she was possessed," he replied while sealing the blunt together with his saliva.

"Shit... let me try to contact her again. It's serious, so y'all get ready for whatever she sets y'all out to do," Ruger voiced sternly.

At that moment, I wanted to know what in the hell did Big Shawn do for him to be tied to the torture device. It had to be some major shit. J-Money was the only one that had talked to X, so I was going to probe more about the situation on Big Shawn being here.

"J-Money, did she say anything else about Big Shawn?" I inquired as I turned around in the brown folding chair to look him in his long, oval-shaped face.

"Nope, but I do recall her sounding as if she'd been crying," he replied before sealing the deal on the second blunt.

"What's the word on Reggio?" Baked asked while placing a blunt to his lips and passed me the second one.

Ring. Ring. Ring.

Ruger's phone rang, and we all looked at him. I was hoping it was my baby calling to say that she was okay and on the way. His response was, "What in the fuck this nigga here wants?"

"Yo," he spat in the phone as he rubbed his bald head.

I studied Ruger's body language, and it was not pleasant. His big eyes grew cold, his lips were tightly pressed together, and the muscles in his jaws clenched and unclenched. Hopping up from the chair, I waltzed to his side because I knew it was some shit that was we getting ready to do. It was apparent that X was in danger. All Ruger said was 'okay,' 'bet,' 'let's set this bait,' and 'get back in touch with me soon as you can, so we can make sure those bitches never breath again.'

When he hung up the phone, Ruger exhaled heavily and said strongly, "Listen up, y'all. That was Juvy. He told me that Reggio is in Miami. He wants Juvy to show him all of X's spots. Reggio wants X dead by all means necessary. We are going to set up a nice play for Reggio and whoever in the way of Chief being alive, understood?"

Baked and J-Money said in unison, "Understood." However, I wanted to know why in the hell Juvy was thrown in the mix. Therefore, I spoke up, "What's in it for him? Why would Reggio come after him?"

"Juvy has been around us for a month. He knows some of X's layouts but not all. He doesn't want any harm brought to her. Juvy wants Reggio dead as well as the family that he grew up with. He said there is a lot of shit that's going on about the 2005 slaying with a hidden person that no one, including Francesco or X, knew about... a lady name Darlene Jockton," Ruger's deep, baritone voice spoke as he looked each of us in the eyes.

"I don't trust that nigga," I spat, placing the blunt to my lips.

"Of course not. He wants the woman that you have," J-Money joked.

Sharply turning my head to look at him, I began to growl before nastily announcing, "He can't fucking have her. I already done claimed that."

As they laughed, none of the guys verbally said a word, and I surely didn't find anything funny. Some minutes passed by and they were still laughing. I wanted to know what was so funny, so I asked.

"What got y'all niggas so tickled?"

"You acting just like them other niggas that she manipulated to get what she wanted. You don' fell for The Golden Pussy, nigga," J-Money chuckled, which caused the other two to hoot and holler.

Not denying anything, I stood with a smirk on my face. I couldn't lie like I didn't fall for that twat between her legs. On the contrary, I loved X as a person first before what fell between her legs. She was extraordinary, all the way around the border!

From a distance, I swore I heard the speakers of The Beast and my heart began to do numbers. Until I quickly thought about The Beast being out of commission since it was banged up pretty bad. Young Thug's "Right Back" played louder, and I knew that The Beast was fixed. Running to the back door of The House of Pain, I heard the fellas joking, and I didn't waste my breath on saying anything to them. Instead, I opened the door and took a step outside to see that pretty black on black car glide perfectly on the cut green grass.

Baby girl knew that was my song, so I jigged to the beat while firing up the blunt. Stepping out of the car wearing a black crop top shirt, black shorts that stopped above the middle portion of her thighs, black gloves, a black bandana perfectly tied around the sides of her pinned up braids, and black steel toe boots, I knew that she was angry as hell. Strolling through the grass with a mean look upon her face, X didn't make an attempt to look at me.

Right then and there, I began to pray that she hadn't found out about Tony yet. The WSFA news channel had mentioned that a body was found on County Road One, and she would know immediately that Ruger had something to do with it because he was the one that was officially appointed to set him free.

Before she walked into The House of Pain, she lifted her head up and yelled, "I'm a billion-dollar bitch off drug dealing!"

Oh, shit, Ruger's ass in motherfuckering trouble. Let me clear the shit up now, I thought as she began to spit angrily, "I think they want a dope girl!"

Knowing what type of mood she was in, I threw the blunt on the ground and ran inside to stand beside the others that were standing in parade rest. She didn't speak to us personally. Instead, she was rapping lines from rap songs. That was everyone's cue that she was not to be fucked with on any level—especially my ass!

"All the niggas wanna do is fuck a dope girl, a dope girl!" she stated as she bounced around on her toes while looking at each of us angrily.

"I guess y'all want my motherfucking position, huh?" she finally yelled after she came to a complete stop and analyzed each of us.

"No, ma'am, Chief," our deep voices spat in unison.

"I can't motherfuckin' tell. I sent y'all on tasks because I knew that y'all could handle it. That's the reason why y'all are a part of The Savage Clique to begin with. I move in a way that others don't; I think outside of the box, on top of the box, inside of the box, and around the fucking box. I asked each of you to do something with clear instructions. I never had a problem from y'all... not a motherfucking one! Two of you thought it was cool to go against what I said, and I'm so not feeling that shit!" she screamed as I swore that I saw the devil horns show on her small head.

"J-Money and Baked, y'all are excused from this conversation. If y'all want to step outside to smoke, y'all are more than welcome," she voiced lightly to them while keeping her eyes on Ruger and me.

How in the hell does she know? I thought at the same time Baked and J-Money said that they were going to stay.

"Why?" she inquired curiously, taking her attention off Ruger and me.

"Once one is in trouble, all in trouble," they announced respectfully.

"Y'all two make me so damn sick," she sniggered while shaking her head. "If y'all must, then y'all must."

Time passed before she said anything to us. She left our asses standing in parade rest until she barked, "Give me thirty push-ups and motherfuckin' sound off with the counts!"

As we did what she commanded, she walked toward Big Shawn and glared at him. She pulled on the black rope to ease the torture device down; once Big Shawn was eye level with X, she whispered something in his ear. He immediately began to shake his head. His jaws were puffing out, and I knew he was trying to talk. The medium-sized red gag ball in his mouth prevented him from talking.

"Thirty!" we shouted out, and she turned to look at us as our chests were up off the ground.

It wasn't anything for us to knock those thirty push-ups out of the way; each morning, we all worked out together.

"Six inches, now!" she barked, waltzing back toward us.

Got damn, X, not the six inches. You know I hate this shit, I thought as we got on our backs and lifted our feet six inches from the ground. I hated that shit the most because it caused a severe burning sensation in the back of my legs and back.

"Ruger and Rondon decided that they wanted to execute Tony against my wishes," she stated loudly as she walked in front of our feet, stopped in front of Ruger and me, glared at each of us, and then continued, "What in the fuck were y'all thinking?"

Ruger and I thought it was a trick question; therefore, we didn't answer. Once she started growling, we knew it wasn't a trick question. Before Ruger could say anything, I hopped on the question.

"I didn't think it was wise to have him still breathing. He knew a lot of shit that we did; he was a key witness to the murder of DB, Gorilla and his family, and that white bitch. I couldn't have him living knowing that. He would put all of us in the electric chair. Once I heard you tell Ruger to let him go and drop him off on Eastern Boulevard, I knew I had to tell Ruger what we really had to do," I stated as I had a hard time keeping my legs from flopping on the ground.

"Are you the chief, Rondon?" she questioned nastily.

"No, ma'am, Chief."

"What is your fucking position, Rondon?" my gorgeous baby mother asked, aggressively.

"I'm one of the four enforcers/bodyguards, financial advisor, and computer hacker," I voiced as my face began to contort from the pain I felt in my back.

"I thought so," she replied and then continued, "Ruger?"

"Yes, Chief," he responded without any indication that he was uncomfortable.

"Are you the chief?"

"No, ma'am, Chief."

"What is your fucking position in *my* organization?"

"I'm one of the four enforcers/bodyguards, Chief. I'm the stalker of a victim and a sharp shooter. I'm your muscle and trusted advisor, Chief," Ruger voiced in his deep, baritone voice while staring into X's beautiful face.

Nodding her head, she said, "Relax."

The sighing from Baked, J-Money, and me caused a light chuckle from X and Ruger.

As she looked amongst us, she shook her head and politely stated, "I wanted to shoot y'all, Rondon and Ruger. There isn't anything that I can do to y'all given the fact that I never had any problems out of you two. From now on, will y'all please listen to me? I do shit for a reason. I actually was going to set J-Money on Tony's ass to see if he was going to open his damn mouth."

Taking a deep breath while looking at Big Shawn, X roughly uttered, "Now, we have an interesting target. The one that I've been looking for since I was fourteen years old."

At the mention of fourteen years old, Ruger sat up and said, "Got damn it... I knew it! Your grandmother, right?"

Nodding her head, X strolled back over toward Big Shawn's chubby, blackened body with Ruger on her heels. Baked, J-Money, and I looked at each other before hopping to our feet. We knew that X's grandmother was killed in a shootout, but we never knew who did it and why. We searched for years without any answers. As

X plucked the gag ball from his mouth, Big Shawn began snitching.

"Tyke came to me with a large amount of money to shoot up Ms. Toole's home. I didn't ask any questions. I never knew that y'all were in the home... until afterwards," Big Shawn stated defensively in a high-pitched tone.

Oh, wow. That nigga, Tyke, was one fucked up individual. Who in the hell would have someone shoot up their mother's crib? What in the hell did Tyke want so damn bad? I thought as I realized that it had something to do with X.

I hoped like hell my conclusion was wrong. I heard many rumors that X's grandmother tried to keep her away from Tyke, and Tyke and his mother were forever arguing about Tyke spending so much time with her.

"Did Tyke have anything over your head?" X asked blankly.

"No."

"Why did my funky ass uncle have my grandmother's home shot up?" X asked sternly as she began to stroll toward us.

Sobbing, the fuck nigga replied, "I honestly don't know. He sent out a task, and I handled it."

That baby mother of mine laughed from the time Big Shawn replied until she disappeared down the hall of the barn.

"Do y'all think that Tyke sent out that hit in order to kill his mother so that he could have full reign over X?" I asked in a low tone.

"That's what I'm thinking," Ruger said as the other guys minus Big Shawn replied, "Yep."

Shaking my head, I quickly cut it short once X came through the barn running full throttle with something in her hands. I wanted to tell her to be careful, but I knew to keep my mouth shut. Soon as she got in front of Big Shawn, she relaxed her right hand, showing the black handle, flush-cut pliers. At the thought of knowing what she was going to do, my stomach started churning. I was okay with seeing blood and shit, but I was not okay with watching a person being mutilated. Not saying one damn word as Big Shawn began to beg X not to do what she was getting ready to do, she clipped the pinky finger off on his left hand and then laughed.

With her right hand, she removed Big Shawn's latest pair of Jordans and the raggedy white sock he had on his right foot. Big Shawn surely began to holler. J-Money started laughing and so did Baked which caused Ruger to laugh. I looked at them niggas like something was wrong with them. Those niggas found anything to laugh at; at that moment, it was the way Big Shawn was hollering and begging. I damn near passed out when X cut off his big toe and the second pinky, but Ruger held me by the top of my denim Levi jeans.

"X, please, please, don't do this to me. I didn't know," Big Shawn cried.

"So... you should've came to me with the knowledge. It's not like you didn't know who was really running the show," she stated as she unzipped the man's pants and pulled out a distorted looking dick. I had a gross look on my face before I dropped my head to the ground. J-Money and Baked started with the jokes that I couldn't laugh at.

"Look at that shit there?" Baked laughed.

"That nigga dick look like it been in World War II," J-Money hollered.

"Mane, you should've threw the whole dick in the garbage can," Baked jested at the same time I glanced up to see what X was doing next.

That motherfucking heifer picked the man's penis up and cut off the head. I fell on the ground at the same time the others reached out for me while laughing. Big Shawn was yelling loudly, and X growled even louder. I didn't see shit else as Big Shawn's timbre pierced my ears. Ruger helped me to the chair, where I tried to zone out from the mutilation show. Baked and J-Money didn't make shit any better because throughout the entire scene, they joked and laughed.

"This cutting off shit is getting boring... hmm, what can I do next?" X asked out loud but not to anyone in particular.

Walking off toward the back of the barn, I couldn't imagine what in the hell she was going to bring back. That sick ass woman of mine came back with a can of kerosene in her hands and a fucking blow torch.

Big Shawn's pained voice began to plead, and X shook her head while tsk-ing before asking the final question, "Who was the shooter?"

"Bango," he whispered.

"Ahh, fuck nawl," Ruger, J-Money, and Baked said in unison as they looked at each other followed by me. Anger soared through me, but I couldn't fix my mouth to curse out Bango.

"I know. I just wanted to see if you were going to tell me the truth," she said as she poured the gasoline on him and sat his ass ablaze.

Stepping back to watch him burn while yelling to the top of his lungs, all of us were looking at her. If I was wondering how in the hell she knew that Bango was the shooter, I knew the others were. We didn't make a move until she did, which was ten minutes after Big Shawn stopped screaming.

As she zoomed toward the back door, so did we. Once outside, I observed the natural scenery. I did that mostly when I needed to avoid asking X a question during a sensitive time. The sun was beaming brightly, there was no wind as birds were flying and enjoying the beautiful, somewhat humid air. A light blue hue graced the sky with minimal clouds visible. The day reminded me of a nice spring afternoon—calm and peaceful. After I was finished analyzing the scene, I had to nudge Ruger. He looked at me and I mouthed, "See how she knew about Bango being the shooter."

Nodding his head, Ruger pulled a cigarette out of his Kool pack and fired it up. He waited a while before he asked the question, and I was antsy as hell to know.

"Chief?" he finally asked, inhaling the smoke from his nicotine stick, causing the jokesters to look at my lady.

"Yes," she replied, looking at him.

"How did you know that Bango was the shooter?"

"He told me," she replied nonchalantly, looking into each of our faces.

Clearing my throat with a raised eyebrow, I wanted to know when in the hell did she talk to him. I didn't have to ask shit because Ruger did for me.

"When did you talk to him?"

"Last night. I met up with him in Clanton."

"So you telling me, you left my motherfucking side for that nigga? Have you lost your damn mind? He could've done something to you?" I shouted as I began to stroll toward her until the fellas grabbed me.

"We had to talk."

"Did you fuck him too?" I clapped back, which made her extremely pissed off.

"If I wanted to, I would've have."

"You bit--," I began to say but was cut off once I realized who I was talking to.

"I'm going to act like you didn't even try to call me out of my name, Reginald," she spat, ambling toward me with her fists balled.

"He's the father of your child, X. Calm down," Ruger said sternly.

"I'm very calm," she replied once she was in my face.

"You got one more time to go against my wishes or try to call me out of my name, and I will send your fucking body to your funky ass mother... understand?" she announced slowly, ensuring that I heard everything that came out of her mouth.

"You can do whatever you want, man. I'm backing all the way off you. There's no way in hell we gonna work out anyways. Let me know when the doctor's appointment is," I told her as I shrugged the fellas off and then continued, "Excuse me, Chief."

"I haven't dismissed you, Rondon."

"Either you are going to dismiss me, or we are going to go at it... you choose?" I voiced angrily as I placed my face close to hers. I tried to walk away until she roughly pulled my shirt and said sincerely, "I didn't fuck him nor did I want to. He wanted to, but I put his ass in his place. Not one time did I disrespect you or us."

"Yeah," I replied before walking off.

"Reginald, I'm serious!" she yelled behind my back.

Hearing my mother's mouth in my head, something in my head snapped, and I turned around quickly. Ruger told me to calm down, but I couldn't. By the time I was in X's presence, I let her ass have it.

"You will not make a fool out of me. You can't do what the fuck you want and think its cool, X'Zeryka. What I'm not going to do is have you doing shit that will jeopardize the well-being of my kid. These last couple of missions, you need to let the fellas handle it. You really are in a vulnerable state... you keep forgetting that you are hormonal as hell. That shit can put us all in jeopardy, mane. I'm going to say what others won't... you ain't fit to be Chief anymore."

Looking at each of us, she asked curiously, "Is that how y'all feel?"

The fellas looked down at the ground and didn't answer until she yelled, "This is my fucking last time asking nicely...is that how y'all feel?"

Nodding their heads, she replied, "Okay. Delete my number out of your phone. I'm officially done with this entire game. I will have y'all final monthly payments in your accounts by tomorrow morning. Do not, and I repeat, do not reach out to me," she stated casually as she strolled into The House of Pain.

"Wow... that did not go as expected," J-Money said in a low tone.

"She's hurt y'all," Ruger replied as he looked toward the torture spot.

"Yes, she is, but she will be okay," I voiced blankly, pulling the blunt from the back of my ear and firing it up.

Moments went by before we said anything. When X finally appeared out of the barn running her ass off, we started sniffing heavily. The stench of wood burning hit the air quickly, and the fellas looked at each other before placing their eyes on X, and she hit the auto start button on The Beast.

"Did you set this place on fire?" I asked her.

She hollered, "Fuck off!"

From her statement and the smell of something burning, we didn't waste any time hustling to our whips and peeling away. By the time we made it to the middle of the field in front of The House of Pain, it exploded. Bits of debris hit the trunk of my car, and I mashed down on the gas pedal.

Ring. Ring. Ring.

As I drove rapidly behind J-Money, I took my phone out of my front pocket and answered X's call.

"Yeah," I voiced.

"We are over. I'm not going to keep the kid. Goodbye, Rondon," she spat in the phone before hanging it up.

Growing angry at her response, I began to growl and curse her out. I was beyond angry, and all I could think about was putting my hands on her.

"Maybe Mama was right... X ain't good enough for me," I thought as I jumped on County Road One and sped past everyone to jump behind The Beast as it flew down the road.

Ring. Ring. Ring.

Briefly looking at the phone before I bent the steep curve on the road, I saw that Ruger was calling. Quickly answering the phone, I said in an agitated tone, "Yo."

"Do not go behind her. Let her be. She's pissed."

"She said she's not keeping my kid, man. I'm real upset about that statement."

"And yet, there's nothing that you can do about it."

Hanging the phone up in his face, I threw it on the passenger floor board and bumped the back of her car. She was going to know that I wanted her ass! As she came to a halt at the stop sign on Highway 82 and County Road One, X jacked The Beast up, made a right turn, and sped off. I was on her ass until she flipped the switch that gave her the ability to make that car do what it do—go super-fast.

Halfway down Highway 82, I lost X, and I had no idea where she went. Pissed at myself, I said fuck it, and called up a freak hoe that would let me take my frustration out on her.

Chapter Fifteen

Bango

I barely got an ounce of sleep once I made it back to my grandmother's, Grandma Toot, house. My thoughts were heavily on the events that led from the time X hopped out of her car, until we left Clanton. My heart and mind did a 360, and I didn't have any intentions of kissing her let alone asking her could I taste that pussy of hers. The conversation and feelings I had for X stopped me from snuggling up with my wife. I didn't know what had gotten into me. The emotions I felt for X when I was younger were back and in full throttle. I truly couldn't understand why. Whenever I looked at X, whether she was crying or not, I felt her pain and anguish. I really felt bad for her and how things really were for her. The one thing I took for granted, she longed for it— love. I was completely out of line from meeting up with X to having lustful thoughts about her. I felt guilty to the point I couldn't hold or look my wife in the eyes.

"Bango, what's wrong? You have been in La-La Land since Grandma Toot brought the twins in here this morning before they left. I'm surprised you didn't hear Markell making all that noise," Taea's soft voice spoke as she walked over toward the bed and took a seat.

"Nothing. I'm just thinking," I told her as I looked at the bronze ceiling.

"A lie ain't shit for you to tell, Marcus Johnson," she replied seductively as she crawled on top of me and began sucking on my neck.

Not in the mood to fuck, I told her, "Chill out, Taea. Daddy not in the mood right now."

"But I am. Doesn't that count for anything?" she questioned as she slid down my body and pulled out my man.

Trying not to raise my voice, I tried a different approach by saying softly, "Taea, I'm not sexually able at this moment. I have a lot of shit going on, and I can't get Daddy up."

Lifting her head up with a smirk on her beautiful, cinnamon-brown face, she replied, "Well, you better get that bitch, X, off your mind. I'm the wife, not her."

Shocked at what she said, I looked down at her and responded with, "Who said anything about her being on my mind?"

"You groaned her name during your little ass catnap, bitch."

"I told you about that bitch shit, Taea," I reminded her for the thousandth time and then continued, "You lying anyways because if I did, you would've been woke my ass up."

Hopping off the bed in a pair of her tight fitting shorts and a white T-shirt, Taea walked to the dark brown, small, circular table in the room and placed her phone in her hand. Scrolling through her phone and pressing one button, my voice boomed as I groaned and moaned X's name.

"Now, what you say again?" my wife inquired with her hands on her hips.

Sitting up in the bed with a quizzical facial expression, I asked, "Why you ain't go off on me?

"Why should I? It's just a dream. I can't do shit about those. However, I can try to stop you from thinking about her, and I know just the remedy."

Delicately planting her phone on the table, Taea seductively removed her clothing. As her clothes landed into a perfect pile on the floor, I gave my gorgeous, five foot six, thick in all the right places wife all of my attention. As she waltzed her behind toward the foot of the bed and provocatively crawled to me, I tried everything in my power to get X off my mind so that I could please my woman. Taea tugged on my black sweatpants, I lifted my body up and let her take the lead. Focusing on the licks that my wife placed on the head of my man, ceased my mind of X.

"Where did Grandma Toot and the kids go, again?" I groaned as my wife brought my man to life. Knowing that Taea needed to moan, that question I had to be asked.

"Her, my grandmother, and the kids are gone to the zoo and then out to eat... so we got the house to ourselves for quite a while," she replied with my harden dick in her mouth.

"Aren't they a little too young for the zoo?" I questioned, enjoying that warm, wet mouth of hers.

"Nope. They are one. They can experience things of that nature," she replied with a mouthful of penis. To this day, I was still amazed and pissed at her abilities to talk with a dick in her mouth.

"Okay," I groaned before pulling her mouth off my member and placing her gently onto her back.

She was in the mood to make love; whereas, I was in the mood to fuck. I hated to disappoint her body, but X's ass was back in my head again. I was angry at her, and since I couldn't punish her, Taea was going to get the business. I didn't waste any time lightly rubbing my mushroom shaped head against her pink, growing bud. As my wife moaned, I politely slid my Johnson inside of the dark, moist, and hot hole.

Slanging the D just the way she like, I felt sick as she moaned that she loved me. Upon hearing her say that, I gave myself a pep talk that things would never get that intense between X and me. As I served my wife some rough loving, I also served myself some harsh words to get over what I was feeling for the one woman that should've been dead. As I put the hammer down on my wife, I vowed never to disrespect or bring harm her way. Loving her soft, passionate groans, I gave my wife all of me until past images of X and I having sex crossed my mind, and I gasped loudly.

"What's wrong?" Taea inquired as she looked into my face.

"A Charlie horse," I lied as I stopped pumping and began to rub my right calf muscle.

"Old ass nigga," my wife snickered while throwing her snatch on my man.

"Chill out, Taea... this pain too much," I growled, not looking at her.

Those past images between X and me were so damn intense. I knew that I had to get the nut out of the way, so that I could focus on the task at hand—getting her out of my life for good. Tired of pretending that I was hurting, I resumed slow stroking that wet monkey of hers. Taea's pussy muscles clenched and unclenched repeatedly and I knew she was close to exploding. Going above and beyond to serve my wife with nothing but the best loving, I told her to get on all fours. I knew that she would be sleep within minutes of us nutting, and I was free to think. Hoping that I would resume pleasing my wife solely because of her, I dived deep so that her voice could drown out X's groans and moans. At first, it worked until Taea moaned a certain way, and my damn mind interpreted that she sounded like X.

Without thinking, I pulled out of her and said, "Fuck!"

"What's wrong, baby?" Taea asked curiously while biting down on her bottom lip and staring at me.

Knowing that my previous sex session with X was on my mind since last night, I knew I couldn't tell Taea what was really wrong.

I was a married man, who shouldn't be thinking about previous sexual partners. I shouldn't have the type of feelings that I possessed for another woman, and I sure as hell wasn't supposed to have asked another woman could I taste her! I was completely fucked up in the brain, and sex with Taea was not a good thing right now.

"I can't do this, Taea. I don't know what is wrong with me. My mind is all over the place, and I'm sorry, baby. I am," I told her as I grabbed my sweatpants off the floor.

"Talk to me, Bango. You are going back into a shell. We can't do that anymore," she voiced lightly, getting off the bed and strolling toward me.

I knew that communication, understanding, honesty, and respect were the keys to a successful marriage, but I couldn't be honest about what I was feeling or thought about. That would cripple us!

"When the time is right, I'll be able to explain things, Taea," I told her, hoping that was enough to shut her up.

"No! Now!" she yelled sternly with her hands on her hips, a raised eyebrow, and a smirk on her face.

Sighing heavily while staring into the face of the one woman that I asked to marry me when I was paralyzed, I could barely fix my mouth to be honest with her. Instead, I stood there while staring into her eyes.

"Bango... speak! Now!" she yelled.

Shaking my head and starting to walk away, she replied softly, "We have faced all the storms together... what is one more that we can face together?"

"I want to fuck X, and that's a problem, Taea. As I'm inside of you, images of her and I keep appearing, and that's wrong, baby. That's fucking wrong," I voiced genuinely, not looking at her.

Turning around slowly to see what she had in her hand, I was relieved to see that she was standing still as her left hand covered her mouth. Taea was quick at grabbing something to throw at me, and the sight of her being completely quiet and still informed me that she was really shook at my revelation. Gasping as she took a seat on the bed, my beautiful wife stared at me with scared, semi-watery eyes. Fully understanding her body language, I began to worry. Exhaling sharply, I strolled to the bed and took a seat beside her. The last thing I wanted to do was hurt her; she was there for me whenever I needed her.

"I need for you to explain things between y'all, Bango," she announced softly while looking at me.

"I'd rather not."

"I'm your best friend first...then your wife. We started out as best friends, in case you forgot. There's not one bitch in this city or the next that I don't know about. How did I not know about X, Bango?"

"I didn't want to tell you about her. The fellas didn't know about her. For me to say anything about how I felt or what her and I did, would've placed me as a target to get robbed. She's not the average female; she's never been. She and I came about around the same time or a little while after you lost your virginity to me. She and I would kick it heavily, and I began to know the ruthless female. What I learned to admire turned into love. Out of nowhere, she disappeared, and when she returned, shit wasn't the same. True enough, we slept together, but when it came down to me wanting to hang out with her, she kicked me out. Basically, after she got her nut, I was gone. I could barely get a 'hi' from her in the same manner that she used to speak to me in. She crippled the shit out of my heart. Taea, I never stopped caring for her well-being."

"Even though she sent Rodrigo to harm me?"

"Rodrigo was only supposed to have scared you... not put his hands on you."

"Says who?" she asked with an attitude.

"X."

Laughing wickedly, Taea spat, "And you believed her?"

"Yes."

"Do I need to file for divorce?"

Taking my time answering the question, I was in deep thought. I didn't know whether to say yes or no. All I knew was that I didn't want to hurt my best friend turned wife because of unfinished business.

"Answer the fucking question, Bango!"

"Hell nawl, don't file for divorce, guh," I finally stated.

"Yeah. The kids and I are heading back to New York first thing in the morning," she replied, hopping off the bed and strolling toward the clothes she had on the floor.

"Why? I thought we were spending Christmas down here?"

"It seems that you need some time to realize what the fuck you got and who you are willing to throw it away for. I'm not that same gullible broad that was your best friend that you actually fucked from time to time, nigga. I'm the smart bitch that's married to you that will take everything that you own, including your fucking soul," she said nicely as she opened the drawer.

With nothing left to say, I flopped back on the bed, stared at that ugly bronze ceiling, and thought about the shit I was going through—all because of X!

***

At 7:00 p.m., we had dinner at Grandma Sue's house. The grandmothers thought it was best to alternate between the two homes during breakfast and dinner. For lunch, we were on our own. Since we've been back in Alabama, a little over eight months, we've also been alternating which grandmother's house we would be living at. Nothing changed in either of their homes other than their furniture and the color scheme of their homes. Our grandmothers lived in Braisedlawn, since we were children. Our grandmothers lived across the street from each other, which gave me easy access to be sneaky with Taea once she lost her virginity to me.

At Grandma Sue's dinner table, it was extremely quiet between my wife and me. Our babies were sleeping comfortably in their bed as usual. I hoped one of them woke up so that I could run to them. The eerie silence between Taea and I drove me insane. I tried everything to get her to engage in a conversation with me prior to dinner, and I failed miserably. I finally gave up and became silent, even though my thoughts were on go mode.

The grandmothers were gossiping about something that happened at their favorite bingo hall, and I shook my head at those hip-hop yapping women. Even the way they discussed shit hadn't changed. Our grandmothers really didn't have a filter, and I hated going out in public with them because I never stopped laughing. The entire time they were talking, they would steal glances at Taea and me. They weren't stupid by a long shot. They knew when something was off between us. They always did. Entertaining the pot roast with carrots and potatoes, French-style green beans, and cornbread, I tried to my best to keep my eyes off Taea. I loved looking at her when she was pissed off and pouting. When she stuck out her bottom lip, I found it extremely adorable. On the contrary, her being upset with me tugged at my heart because I knew she was very unsure about us, and that was something that I didn't want. I always wanted her to be one-hundred percent sure about us—even when I wasn't sure.

Since we've been in Alabama, we have been bumping heads. Of course, it was about X and how quickly I can handle my end. There was no way I could tell her that I didn't want to kill her because of an intuition I had. That one word, *intuition*, would've caused a massive argument I was clearly not up for!

"The kids and I are heading back home in the morning," Taea stated as she popped a potato into her

petite mouth while eyeing our grandmothers.

"Why?" the grandmothers asked. At the same time, they turned their heads to look at me.

"We have to get on with our lives, and I can't run a company from down here."

"I understand that, Taea," Grandma Toot said, still looking at me with a smirk on her face.

Taea owned Johnson R&D, which was a research and development company that specialized in rare diseases such as Familial Adenomatous Polyposis. She had a thing for science, and illnesses that specialists and scientists couldn't wrap their brains around. I was so proud of her nerdy ass for finally chasing her dreams. Soon as we were turned twenty years old, I had to nag her about speeding up the process. Of course, she gave me thousands of excuses as to why she wasn't ready.

It was nothing like owning your business versus to working for someone else. During the early stages of my recovery, I ran Taea's idea by my father, which caused him to nag her more than I did. Within two months of my recovery, Taea had her business plan, location, and was in the process of hiring for Johnson R&D. My father was her number one sponsor. As soon as people saw his name tied into the company, more people signed on the dotted lines.

Ring. Ring. Ring.

My phone knew how to save me from the pits of hell, and I was very grateful for it going off! Pulling it out of my back pocket, I exhaled heavily upon seeing my father's name displayed across the screen. Right then, I wished that it would've not went off. I was not in the mood to deal with his rants about killing X. Excusing myself from the dinner table, I didn't answer the phone until I closed the front door behind me.

"Hello," I breathed into the clear, chilly night's air.

"Where are you?" my father's husky, deep Italian voice spoke.

"At Taea's grandmother's house," I stated as I walked to the edge of Grandma Sue's beautifully decorated front yard.

"I'm bringing the battle to Alabama. Tell Taea to get the kids out of the state and go back home."

Aggravation appeared immediately before I said, "Leave X alone, Dad. Let the shit be dead. Whatever Tyke told you was a damn lie. The man had his own mother killed and lied to X about it. What makes you think he didn't lie to you about the same *niece* that took his organization and perfected it."

"It's apparent that you are just like your mother— fall for what's between a person's legs rather than who they are," he said nastily before blowing air out of his mouth.

The mentioning of that bitch's name drove me to go the fuck off!

"You know what? I'm so fucking tired of you thinking you know me. Well, guess what, Reggio Esposito... you don't! Don't ever compare me to a bitch that you and your family destroyed. Listen carefully. You fuck with X... the consequences will be dire, and you can bet your last fucking dollar on that!"

Chapter Sixteen

X

It was 7:30 p.m. when I finally made it to headquarters and guess who was waiting on me when I pulled up? None other than Rondon. I instantly put on the 'don't fuck with me' facial expression. I wasn't in the mood to hear him nagging about what I said about not continuing the pregnancy. True enough, being in this state made it hard for me to complete my tasks, but deep down, I really couldn't bring myself to be sound about the completion of killing Bango. He's never done anything to me other than showing me what love feels like.

"You okay?" Rondon asked, standing in a pair of dark, khaki pants, a white-collared shirt, and a pair of sparkling white, high-top Radii Jax.

"Yeah," I stated in a low decibel as I approached the porch and avoided eye contact.

After I unlocked the front door, we walked in, and I headed straight to the refrigerator. I was glad he wasn't bugging or even trying to hold a conversation with me. The less we spoke to each other the better things would be between us. The last thing either of us needed was to say or do something that we would regret. At this particular time, all I wanted to do was sit back and chill. I had a thousand things to do since my goons felt that I wasn't fit to be chief anymore. I had to prove to them that just because I was pregnant, didn't mean I couldn't run my organization.

"Are you hungry?" Rondon asked, walking up behind me.

"Yeah," I voiced dryly.

"What do you want to eat?" he replied as he kissed me on the right side of my neck.

"Not sure yet."

"I didn't mean to hurt your feelings today at The House of Pain. I didn't try to step on your toes. I just want what's best for our child and you. I would never want anyone to jeopardize what I have placed inside of your womb."

"Okay," I said nonchalantly.

"Why are you talking to me so dryly, X?" he probed, turning me around to face him.

"No reason. Just don't want to talk right now," I told him as I stared at his neck.

"Go sit down and let me fix us something to eat. Okay?"

"Yeah," I replied, walking away from him.

Taking a seat on the black leather sofa in the front room, I analyzed everything that I loved about the manufactured home. I designed it so that it wouldn't look like an ordinary trap house. I bought expensive African artifacts because I loved African culture and their heritage, thanks to Tyke sending me there as my punishment. Every inch of the three-bedroom trailer had a different color mixed with gold. Furniture was simple yet elegant. I had this thing where I had to be comfortable no matter where I placed my ass. Growing tired of analyzing the next place I was going to set ablaze, I logged into Facebook.

As I hopped on the 'Book, I hoped that I would get a hearty laugh since I was in desperate need of one. I had two pages that I networked off, so I checked the first one. The people that I had on it weren't talking about anything. Therefore, I logged out and hopped on the second one. My second page was on beast mode. Old and new messages were on wham, niggas trying to holler, my peoples wanting to know have I seen Truk (you best to believe they didn't have my number), and a message from Marsha Monroe— Tony's mother. I knew then that it was either going to be some shit, or it was going to be a sad moment, so I braced myself for what she had to say. As I opened the message, I prayed that Marsha wasn't going to say shit that was going to piss me off and have her on the kill list.

Marsha Monroe: *Hey, X. I didn't have your number and neither did Landon. I was informing you that Tony's funeral will be held on Wednesday at 11:00 a.m. at Royce and Johnson Funeral Home.*

Seeing the final arrangements for Tony had tears sliding down my face. Not in the mood to have a blow up with Rondon, I quickly wiped my face and responded to her message. However, it was going to happen the moment I placed eyes on Tony's dead corpse. Rondon and Ruger did the most when they killed him, and I haven't properly laid into their asses.

MsToole2U: *I'm sorry for your loss, Marsha. Thank you for reaching out to me. I will be there. Do you need anything? Food? Help with funeral arrangements?*

She wasn't online, but I was sure her money hungry ass was going to respond, and I wasn't going to give her ass a dime of my money; I was very sure that Tyke's funky ass left the bitch some money.

"How do you feel about a filet mignon, sautéed asparagus with cheese, and rice pilaf?" Rondon's voice boomed, interrupting my thoughts.

"Kill the rice pilaf... I'll be fine with mashed potatoes," I said, not looking at him.

"Bet."

Ding. Ding.

A text from the number Bango called me on piqued my interest. Therefore, I rapidly opened the message to see what he had to say.

474-854-9898: *I need to see you. Are you free anytime soon?*

Me: *No. I'm not in the mood to talk tonight.*

474-854-9898: *My father is coming to Alabama, and he's seeking you.*

Me: *That's fine. He's coming to the right place. I'm not hiding. Tell him all of my locations.*

474-854-9898: *I'm not against you, X'Zeryka. I never was.*

Me: *Goodbye Marcus.*

474-854-9898: *I really need to see you!*

Not responding to the last text, I deleted the entire thread and thumbed through Facebook. Smiling at the somewhat funny memes I ran across took my mind off the shit I was going through. Halfway through scrolling, anger rose in me, the palms of my hands became sweaty, and I cleared my throat several times.

"You need some water?" Rondon asked while he placed butter, onions, mushrooms, and bell peppers into a skillet that was sitting on a stove.

"Nawl," I replied nastily as I read every damn comment under a photo.

Oh, wow. So, is this how we really going to do shit? I inquired as I tried to check myself while gathering a shit load of evidence. Once I read every comment and gathered all the evidence I needed, I was off the sofa and ambling toward the side of the kitchen counter where Rondon was preparing dinner.

"Sooooo, what the fuck is this?" I asked him as I held up the picture of him at some random hoe's house hours prior.

Looking at the picture, he shook his head and stared at me.

"So, you telling me that you have nothing to say?" I replied casually.

"I was chilling with some people from the hood, X. There was a house full of people. Don't make shit out of nothing, okay, baby?" he stated blankly.

As soon as he was done, I scrolled up to the bitch's caption and shoved the phone in his face as I politely read the chick's caption, "Chilling with dat black babi. I love me some Rondon."

"Let me explain—" he began to say before I knocked everything on the counter onto the floor and picked up the steak knife.

"Hear me loud and clear. Get the fuck out of this trap house. Don't come around me, trying to talk to me. We have absolutely nothing to talk about. You with the games, and I'm not up for it. Here I was thinking that you were truly looking out for my best interest, but you really trying to knock me off the throne. I was leaving the game anyways. I am tired of doing this shit. Now, get the fuck out of here before I really send your parents your body."

Knocking the steak knife out of my hand, Rondon shoved me gently into the corner of the counter and voiced sternly, "That girl means nothing to me, X. She was just a piece of ass when I'm frustrated. I fucked her because you made me mad when you said that you were going to terminate the pregnancy. I was fucking pissed off, and I wanted to run you off the road."

Hearing him say that he fucked her had tears sliding down my face, as I tried to push him away from me. On the contrary, I couldn't figure out why I was so upset with him. I should've been upset with myself for allowing things to go so far between us. All I kept hearing was Ruger saying, "You are green, X. You know nothing about feelings for lust and love. Take your time with the matters of your heart."

"Whatever we are trying to have is over. I don't want this anymore. Shit, I'm not sure if I ever wanted it. You forced this fuckship upon me. If it's the streets you want, be my guest and have at it. Now, leave. We have nothing else to talk about," I spat, staring him in the face.

"I don't want to leave, X. I need you to see that I want you and only you," he pleaded as he tried to rub my stomach, but I quickly knocked his hand away from me.

"You should've thought about that before you stuck your dick in another female when you proclaim that you loved and wanted only me. So, I guess it's cool for you to stick your dick in someone when you are frustrated with me and come in my face like shit ain't even happen, huh?"

"No, that's not what I'm saying," he stated as he placed his hands on my twat and rubbed on it.

I lost my entire mind and bust that bitch in the face with my head. Before I knew it, he was tussling to get me off him as I brought my feet, hands, head, and anything that I could grab at his body. Not giving a damn about the pregnancy, I returned back to "that" X and gave him the fight of his life. Slicing his arm with the steak knife that I snatched off the floor, Rondon rushed me and slammed me on the floor. With anger in his eyes, he bent down and spat, "You gon' learn when to submit to me, X'Zeryka!"

"I'm not a fucking dog, bitch! I ain't submitting to a motherfucking thing... especially a nigga that can't keep it real!"

"This is my last time telling you to watch your mouth. I'm not one of your victims," he voiced as he began to slide his hands up my dress.

"Mane, if you don't get the fuck away from me. I'm really going to do something to you," I voiced in an upset tone.

Pushing his hands out of the way, I plowed my head into his for the final time.

"Ahh shit, X. I swear when my head stops hurting, I'm going to give you what the fuck you been asking for," he shouted as he backed away from me.

Standing against the marbled countertop with his head upwards, I hollered for him to get the fuck out.

"I ain't going no damn where, man. We are going to talk this shit out. Now, chill until I get this pain under control."

Not hearing anything that he had to say, I jumped up and ran toward the drawer that held the bigger knives. As I strolled toward him with hurt in my eyes, pain in my heart, and tears sliding down my face, I held the knife firmly as I skated to his body. Dropping his head down to look at me, Rondon yelled, "Get the fuck on with that knife, X!"

"Get the fuck out... or I will have to use it."

He saw that I wasn't backing down. He let me come close to him only for his hands to be placed around my neck as he applied pressure to it. Taking my right leg and kicking him in the stomach, didn't do what I thought it would.

"Drop the fucking knife, X," he demanded, glaring into my eyes.

"Get out," I whispered, gazing back into his.

Kicking him in the dick was the reason why his hand left my neck, which enabled me to land punches to his face and head; when the pain subsided from his private area, that nigga gave me a real battle. As he pulled me by the front of my dress, I continued to throw punches on his body.

"Rondon, let my shit go and fucking leave, nigga!"

"You fucked that nigga, Juvy, on more than one occasion, but you get mad at me for fucking a hoe when I'm pissed off at you! Mane, fuck what you talking about!" he yelled as he yanked on the dress, bringing me closer to him. Once I was in close proximity of him, he shoved my body on the table and spread my legs with his knees.

"No the fuck you ain't thinking that you finna fuck me! I don't know where all that dick been, and you been fucking me raw!" I spat nastily as I tried to push him away from me.

Knowing that I could manipulate my body to do whatever I wanted to, Rondon made damn sure to hook his left arm in between the back of my right leg while his right hand unzipped his pants, which fell to the ground. With my left leg, I kicked him in the chest. After I roughly kicked him, Rondon continuously brought his right hand down on my thighs until I cried out.

"Keep your fucking feet to yourself, X," he replied as he freed his dick from his plaid blue, white, and gray boxers.

"You are fucking trying to rape me... you damn right I'm finna defend myself, nigga!" I sobbed, angrily.

"Ain't nobody finna rape you, guh," he laughed while rubbed the head of his dick on my thigh and leg.

"Look at what you are doing, Rondon! This is some rapist shit, guy!"

Pinching my right thigh hard, Rondon talked harshly to me. The more he talked, the more I hated that I didn't put a bullet in his head. Trying to block out the pain that he was rendering to my body didn't help once he decided to pinch and twist the skin that was in between his thumb and index fingers.

"Oucccch!" I yelled out at the same time I lost the fight of keeping him away from The Golden Pussy.

"Good little girl," he chuckled at the same time he slid my body down the table and dove head first in my girl.

Not wanting his mouth anywhere near me quickly changed once he started making me nut back to back. However, the feeling of being played never left my mind and that was the reason why I pushed his head away from me and tried to get free. With his hands around my ankles, he gripped tighter and pulled my pussy all the way into his face. One strong flicker of his tongue, and I hollered, "Ronnndoonn."

"Let me handle my business, so I can resume to cooking us dinner while you take a nap," he hummed against my clit while he inserted two of his fingers.

"I don't want this anymore. Leave me alone!" I begged as my back arched, and I squirted on his face and hands.

"I'm not going anywhere," he barked in my pussy which made me coo his name.

"I never wanted you, Rondon... never!" I yelled at the same time my back arched, and I swore it damn broke.

Hopping up from in between my legs with a mouthful of my juices, Rondon was angry. His entire body language showed that he was beyond pissed by my statement. I quickly regretted saying I didn't want him. Not knowing what to do but to observe him and hold onto my boss bitch posture, I gave him an eye for an eye.

Glaring into my eyes as if he wanted to kill me, Rondon slammed his man inside of me. Pain rippled through my vagina as the hurtful groan escaped from my throat. That guy rode me until I couldn't speak. My mouth was dry, pussy was aching while he was still inside of me, and my toes and hands hurt from me having them balled so tightly. The entire time he was roughly fucking me, he was talking nastily and not in a sexual way. He let me know that he was pissed with my comment. He clearly stated how much he hated Juvy and what he was going to do to him.

My body ached from the unwanted services Rondon was putting on it. It seemed like it took him forever to get done with me.

When he finally did nut, stuffed his dick back into his boxers, and pulled up his pants, that motherfucker gazed into my eyes and spat angrily, "Now, bitch, I can leave. Thanks for the fuck."

With my upper torso stretched on the table, legs open so that some air could hit my worn out, sore pussy, back feeling as if it was on fire, and tears streaming down my face, I laid on that damn table with a priceless look upon my face. All I could do was watch him walk out of the door and feel sorry for myself. The way I was feeling, I knew there could never be a way that Rondon and I could ever be. He made me feel worse than my deceased uncle Tyke did, and I couldn't have that type of person in my life.

After some time, I hobbled off the kitchen table and ambled toward the master bathroom. Upon the completion of drawing a warm bubble bath, I soaked and cried. I cried for the way I was feeling, I cried for the embryo I was pregnant with, I cried for choosing this life, I cried for being a smart individual but having a weak mind, and I cried for my grandmother! I cried until I couldn't anymore.

Chapter Seventeen

Taea

Tuesday, December, 19th

The weather in New York City was very disrespectful and rude. I had never been in the city during winter time, and I was ready to flee my ass back to Alabama. Any other time, I wouldn't have missed my birth state, but the way New York weather was set up, a sister was in need of the bipolar weather from the south. I could barely shop in peace for the speeding wind and wet snow.

Since the twins and I have been home, I've been swamped with Christmas shopping and worrying about my marriage to the point that I couldn't enjoy the holiday season with my babies. Bango told me before we left that everything would be alright, but deep down, I really didn't believe it. It was different being his wife versus his best friend. I had to endure things differently. What he saw wasn't a threat; I saw it as a big threat! I wasn't up for any bitches thinking they could come into my relationship. I was always ready to bat a bitch down about my husband and children. As his best friend, I wasn't up for the fighting and drama. In the past, I would dismiss his ass for a week or two until he popped up at my crib and then we would be okay. As his wife, I couldn't dismiss him. I had to deal with it all but also not be a stupid individual for him.

Marcus "Bango" Johnson and I lived across the streets from each other from birth until we got our cribs. Grandma Sue and Grandma Toot lived across from each other before we were even born, so in my mind, it was meant for us to be best friends. Bango and I had so much in common. For starters, our grandmothers raised us. Neither of our mothers wanted anything to do with us because of a man. Bango knew his father, whereas I didn't. Reggio was in Bango's life but not the way that he wished. Bango wanted a father figure that was proud to show him off to his family. True enough, Reggio looked out for Bango since the day he was born, but that wasn't enough in my husband's eyes.

We loved video games, coloring, and painting. During our adolescent years, Bango was the one that told me what to do when I first started having periods. He was my first love and heartache. I endured so much by being his best friend that it made my head spin. Through all the hell he had coming my way, he made sure that I was straight. He was the reason why Johnson R&D was up and running within two months of his recovery from being shot twice in his left rib cage. Truth be told, I was a mess, and I knew there was no way I could run a company. I was too worried and scared for my husband's life. Signing checks was the least of my worries; having a living, healthy husband was my main priority. The day of our wedding changed me, and I tried not to let it but it did.

After Bango fully recovered from his wounds from an assault rifle's bullet that that bitch, X, put into his body, I still didn't understand how he kept letting the chick slip through his hands! It literally irked my nerves. I knew one motherfucking thing— if that nigga don't come back with an obituary, he and I were for sure going to get a divorce. I wasn't going to have it any other way! That girl was despicable, and I didn't want her breathing another moment, so of course, before I left I gave him an ultimatum—her or his family.

Ring. Ring. Ring.

Grabbing my phone out of the front pocket of my jacket, I wondered what Gonzilla, my nanny, wanted. Sliding my gloved finger across the screen of my phone, I answered politely, "Hello."

"Hi. Mrs. Johnson, I was calling to inform you that I have a family emergency, and I will not be able to tend to Markell and Martaea for the next two days," she spoke softly in a preppy voice— the voice I hated dearly but grew to deal with.

"I hope everything is alright, Gonzilla. Call me if you need anything, okay?" I told her as I finished up the last of my shopping in Wal-Mart.

"Thank you, Mrs. Johnson," she replied before we ended the call. Gonzilla Marisole was a twenty-year-old, half white and half Mexican woman that I met one day as I strolled through the vegetable and fruit aisle in C-Town Supermarket. She and I clicked over how attentive she was the twin girls she was pushing in a double-seated stroller. We chatted for a while, which led her to tell me that her assignment with the children's family was ending since she wasn't able to move across the U.S. with them. I had been in search of a nanny for two weeks with no luck; therefore, I had to ask her to come aboard and help me with the twins. She's been in our lives way before the twins were born. She helped me learn a lot about being a mother. Honestly, Gonzilla was more than an employee; she was my friend.

After I placed my cellular device back into its rightful place, I glanced over my shopping list. Once I realized that everything was checked off, I was anxious to get off the sugar and flour aisle. As I backed the packed buggy, I bumped into someone.

Not paying attention to the person after I apologized, the familiar voice said, "Excuse me, lady... long time no see."

Spinning around on my heels to face the woman, a widespread smile came across my face as I stared the gorgeous Kutta down.

Walking inches to her with outstretched arms, I spoke happily, "Hey, honey. How are you?"

"I'm fine and you?" she replied as she flipped her long, straight, jet black hair away from her face.

"I'm good. Let me go ahead and lay your ass out right now," I laughed and then continued, "You have my address, so why haven't you come by personally to drop the money off, heifer?" I inquired curiously with my hands on my hip.

With a dumbfound look upon her face, she questioned, "Money? You know you better explain that."

Her facial expression threw me off, and I knew I had to see why it was as if she didn't know what I was talking about. As I was about to explain, there were a couple of people walking up and down the main aisle. I moved my buggy out of the way. While I was doing that, Kutta's five foot four, thick body frame moved along. Kutta was the total definition of bad. She wore nothing but the latest designer clothing and bags. Her nails and jewelry were on fleek. I guaranteed that her whip was bedazzled just like the owner. I never knew much about Kutta because Bango didn't know much about her—so he said. All I knew was that she came from money, and that he met her through Eric, a once upon a time, deceased best friend.

"So, you telling me that you weren't the one sending me money after the fake death of Bango?" I asked with a raised eyebrow.

"Now, bitch, we finna walk around Wal-Mart because you are telling me something that I didn't even know about," she voiced in a low tone as she placed her left hand to her mouth.

Leaving the aisle, I gave her the rundown on what happened to Bango on our wedding day, and I was sure to let her know who was responsible.

"How was his recovery?" she asked as we passed the baby section.

"It was really hard, honey. He went through the worst depression ever. He couldn't understand why that bitch would shoot at him when she clearly had chances prior to our wedding. Then, the hunt started, and that damn near drove me insane."

"The hunt?" she probed curiously.

"Girl, him, his father, and his father's goons went on a hunt for X. Now, check this out, Bango been found the bitch but never ceased her from breathing. We've seen her on more than ten occasions, and that nigga would not knock that hoe off."

"Wow! Y'all have been through a lot, Taea. Now, to this money... why would you think that I would send you money?" she questioned quickly not truly responding to what I told her.

"Bango always told me that if anything ever happened to him, that you would be the one that would send money," I told her as I came to a complete stop in front of the electronics department.

"Honey, I didn't even know any of that shit happened. I was home in Russia. The last time I saw Bango was in June of last year. When we parted ways, I changed numbers and went back home. I came back to the States yesterday."

"So, who in the hell was sending me money then?" I asked myself more so than her.

"Did Bango know about the money being sent?"

"Yes."

"What did he say, or what was his facial expression?"

"He shook his head, lightly smiled which faded away quickly, and mumbled I hate that fucking brown bitch."

Kutta's facial expression was priceless as I told her what my husband said upon knowing that money was being sent—after his fake death. Her eyes grew big, and she bit down on the right side of her bottom lip as if she was trying to avoid saying anything. As I stared at Kutta, I knew damn well that Bango wasn't referring to her as a brown bitch since Kutta was a high yellow chick. By me being a people's person, I knew something wasn't right. Her body language was off; therefore, I asked her what was up.

"Nothing," she stated in a high-pitched tone. She was lying through her pretty white, straight teeth, and I was becoming very agitated.

"Kutta... do you know who could've sent the money? Your reaction to what Bango said got me a little throwed off."

"No, I don't know who could've sent you that money, Taea. Honey, I wouldn't even worry about it. Shit, spend the money and keep it moving," she tried to joke, but I wasn't in a joking mood.

"Is there something I need to know, Kutta?"

"Taea, leave the shit alone. The last thing you need to do is go up against that bitch. You know how Bango is about you, so please leave that tree alone."

"What the fuck is up with everyone telling me not to bark up that tree? She is a bitch just like me!"

"If you never listen to anything I say, please leave that woman alone. She is not to be fucked with on any levels. I'm not telling you something that I don't know."

"Is she capable of sending me the money?" I probed, ignoring the advice she gave me.

"Yep. She's capable of anything."

"Did she send me the money?"

"Taea, I gotta go. You getting into some shit I'm not up for. It was nice seeing you. Tell Bango I said hello," she said quickly before giving me a hug and jogging down the aisle.

While I watched Kutta walk away, I was shaking my head and fuming at the same time. With a shaky hand, I snatched my phone out of my front coat pocket and dialed Bango's number. The phone went to voicemail, which caused me to dial the number again. I dialed his number three more times before I left a brief, nice/nasty voicemail.

"What I bet not find out is that hoe, X, sent me money thinking that you were dead, and yo' motherfuckin' ass knew about it!"

***

"Aww, why are you doing all of that fussing, Little Miss Martaea?" I asked my chunky bundle of joy as she cried.

As I lightly squeezed her jaws, I applied the baby Oral gel to the bottom of her back gums. I was glad when she was done cutting teeth. Markell cut his teeth, and we didn't have any problems with him fussing as much as Martaea was.

"Hopefully, you'll be feeling better soon, sweetheart," I told her after I placed her on my chest, followed by gently rubbing her back.

"Forever" by R. Kelly blared through the speakers of my phone, and my heart began to beat rapidly. It was 9:00 p.m., and my husband was just calling me. If he didn't think I wasn't going to serve him a mouthful of curse words, he was sadly mistaken. As I answered my phone, I rolled my eyes.

"Hello," I sighed into the phone.

"What y'all doing?" he asked.

"Markell sleeping. Martaea in the process of going to sleep," I voiced in a nonchalant timbre. I made sure to not mention anything about me. If he was going to act in a way that made me not want to be with him, he had to get used to me not answering his questions when it concerned me.

"Ahh."

With as much attitude as I could muster, I said, "Umm, so did you get my voicemail?"

"Yeah," he replied, dryly.

I hated when anyone talked or said something to me in a dry manner. That shit set me the fuck off. However, I couldn't go off with my children in my presence. So, I remained halfway calm, but I was surely going to get my answers.

"Okay, so where is my response?" I stated curtly.

"Mane, Taea, where are you getting your theories from?" he huffed.

"Ain't no way in the hell you finna answer me with a question. Either you going to answer the question, or I'm hanging up the phone and not answering until you do. How 'bout those cookies?"

"No, she did not send me the money. Kutta sent it," he lied, and I was fuming like fuck.

"You got one more chance to tell me who in the hell sent me that money, Marcus Johnson."

"I told you Kutta, baby. I have no reason to lie."

Oh no, this bitch did not say that, I thought as I counted to ten because I was ready to snap.

"Baby, you there?" my lying ass husband asked.

"Hell yes, I'm here with your lying ass. For your information, Kutta didn't send the money. I saw her in Wal-Mart today, and she was dumbfounded as fuck when I asked her why she never hand delivered the money. It was very cute how she reacted to what you said and did when I told you about the brown envelope after those two guys dropped it off." When we fake declared Bango as dead, the very first person that delivered money was a light-skinned guy. He dropped off a fat envelope filled with money every month. Then, he was replaced by a dark-skinned guy.

The line was quiet as hell, and I knew then that he really knew who sent the money, and that angered me more.

"Did X send the money, Bango?"

Finally, he replied, "Yes."

"You must think this shit is a joke, dude. I tell you what I'm not finna deal with is your past with a bitch that damn near killed your ass twice. Why does she have such a hold on you? Do you want to be with her? You know what... don't even worry about answering any of those questions, man," I spat before hanging up the phone and powering it off.

I was past pissed off, and I didn't want to say anything that I would regret. Thus, I had to cease the call. My children were sleeping comfortably, and I badly needed R&R. After I placed them in their room, I retreated to Bango's and my bathroom.

I was frustrated and feeling like a damn fool once again. At times, I felt like the only reason why he asked me to be his wife was because he was paralyzed from the waist down. I really think that if he and X hadn't gotten into that shootout months prior to our wedding, he would've never asked me to marry him when he was lying up in one of UAB's hospital rooms. As I thought about things, I felt like he knew those random hoes he was fucking around with wasn't going to look after him like I would because I was his best friend.

While I thought about all the shit I've been through with him, good and bad, I was hurt as the bad slammed into my head-- repeatedly. Trying to avoid thinking about the things that took place, I ran some hot bath water and placed a nice amount of bath beads into the tub. Once I turned off the water, the quietness of the bathroom and my thoughts ran rampant. I became sad as I thought about my husband telling me that he wanted to fuck a bitch that almost ceased his life.

The tears rolled down my face as I wondered what was with the chick and what was wrong with me that he had the desire to sleep with another woman. Feeling horrible about the situation and not wanting to get my feelings bashed no more than what they already were; I knew there was only one thing to do—seek a divorce.

Chapter Eighteen

Rondon

I lost my mind as I tried to contact X. She didn't answer any of my texts, calls, or social media messages. I rode past all of her houses and the trap house on several occasions to see if she was there. To my surprise, I didn't see anyone at her properties either time I went by there, and I was really pissed the fuck off. In my heart, I hoped she didn't terminate the pregnancy. I knew I was dead wrong for what I said to her, but she made a nigga mad as fuck with that smart as comment she made. I was even wrong for fucking ole girl when I proclaimed that I loved X. I couldn't accept the fact that I did wrong and asked for forgiveness. Instead, I did what most niggas did—made a damn excuse.

"Are you spending the night again?" Jacquel asked, interrupting my thoughts.

"Nope."

"You been over here for the past two nights. What's up with you?" she probed, coming to sit down beside me.

"Nothing," I lied, sliding further down the sofa.

"The bitch you been trying to get threw you to the curb, huh?" she laughed.

"Watch your mouth, bitch," I snapped, looking into her light-skinned face, which was filled with makeup that didn't match her skin tone. Once again, I was in the wrong for staying over the same bitch's house that put me on Facebook. The only reason why I was over there was because the dumb bitch let me trap and cook dope out of her project home for only fifty dollars. So, why not use the idiot?

"I'm just saying," she continued, trying to touch my leg.

Damn, I wish she would stop talking and touching on me because I'm 'bout ready to shoot her in the face and set the house on fire, I thought as I had a mean grimace on my face.

"Mane, don't touch me," I told her nastily while placing my phone on the holster and snatching up my keys that were lying on a dirty, broken down glass table.

"My period late, Rondon," she blurted out with a smirk on her face.

Exhaling heavily, I stared at the idiot with a smile on my face. I knew it wasn't going to be long before she came with that bullshit, thinking she was going to lock me down. Only one person was capable of locking me down, and she was already pregnant by me. I knew for sure that Jacquel's pregnancy wasn't because of me, so the best thing she could do was find that baby's pappy.

"Did you tell the father?" I chuckled, standing up.

"I'm telling him now," she stated with an attitude.

"I'm not the father of that baby. The only person that is pregnant by me is *my* Chief. So, you can miss me with that shit," I stated, strolling toward the brown stainless steel doors that all housing authority properties installed in their units.

"You are the father; you were the only one I was fucking around with," she said in a high-pitched tone as she got up to walk behind me.

Turning around on the heels of my Timbs, I voiced sternly, "I used rubbers with you, guh. Like I stated before, go and find that baby's pappy because I'm not that nigga."

"Just get ready to be a father to this child, sir," she replied, walking back toward the worn out, brown suede sofa.

For a while, I stood there and stared the dumb broad. I wanted to choke her ass out, but instead, I laughed heavily and turned around while shaking my head. Before I opened the door to leave her establishment for good, I made sure that she understood what I was saying.

"You come at me again about a pregnancy that I didn't contribute to, I will fuck you up. Don't test me. You really don't know what type of nigga I am. Keep on fucking with me, and you will surely see how black my ass is!"

While I was walking to the car and laughing about Jacquel's stupid statement, my phone rang. Snatching it off the holster, I looked down to see that Baked was calling.

"Yo," I answered.

"What's the move for this lovely Monday, nigga?"

"Shit, I can't call it. Mane, have you heard from X?" I asked as I opened the driver's door of my candy apple red 2016 Challenger and slid in the comfortable black seat.

"Nawl, we been trying to reach her. All of our calls are going straight to voicemail. Ruger 'bout to lose his entire damn mind trying to figure out where in the hell she at."

"I'm on the same level as Ruger, mane."

"How in the hell can we make sure that she is safe?"

"No damn idea. She is completely off the grid, and you know how that is. I gotta find her, man. I fucked up, bruh."

"Oh, I know. I saw it. Congratulations on another successful pregnancy, mane. Chief, sho' nuff finna show her entire ass," he said before laughing. Hoping like hell he was joking, I had to ask him what he was talking about.

"Some chick just posted a picture of you, her, and a positive pregnancy test online."

"Woe, I know you lying?" I asked heated.

"Nope."

"I'm finna kill this bitch. That hoe lying. The only person I got pregnant is X," I stated as I got out of the car and ran back to Jacquel's front door.

"Mane, are you running?"

"Hell fuck yes...back to this dumb broad's house... she finna take that fraudulent ass shit down or get beat the fuck up one."

"Bruh, you wild," he said, laughing and then continued, "You rolling with J-Money and me tonight?" he inquired, inhaling what was probably a blunt at the same time I banged on the bitch's door.

"Who is it?" Jacquel asked in a fake, white woman's voice.

"Bitch, open this motherfuckin' do'!" I yelled as I began to kick on it.

In the background, Baked was laughing and talking shit. Ignoring him, I kept telling the dumb chick to open up but she refused.

"Just know you just ended your fucking life, hoe. Running around this bitch talking about I got you pregnant. You lost your entire damn mind, Jacquel. I'mma fix yo' ass... best to believe that," I shouted as people began to stop or come out of their project homes to see what was going on.

Walking away from the hoe's house, I asked Baked, "Where y'all talking about going?"

"Club Magic."

"Yeah, I'm down," I replied as I popped my neck.

"A'ight. We can either meet up at the club or jump in one ride. You make that call."

"Bet. I'll holla at 'cha later on."

"A'ight," he said before hanging up the phone.

Once I made it to my car, I started the engine and peeled away from Patterson Court. I was in need of finding X. I had to make things right with her. I didn't know where to begin looking for her, and then it dawned on me that she was probably mourning that fuck nigga Tony. Last Wednesday, I went to the nigga's funeral in hopes of seeing her there, but I didn't. As I pretended to show my final respects to the bitch nigga, I looked through the visitor's log, and I saw her name on the first page. Growing angry at the thought of her showing respects to a motherfucker that she was once head over heels in love with, I fled Royce and Johnson Funeral Home pissed the fuck off.

For the next two hours, I rode around Montgomery trying to locate any of her cars, and I didn't find it. Therefore, I gave up and hit the interstate, heading back to my home in the lovely community of Silver Hills in Prattville. As I pulled into my driveway, my phone began to ring from one of my college buddies, Drew McKenzie.

"What's up, buddy?" I piped into the phone after I slid my right index finger across the phone with my ear nowhere near the phone.

"Shit, man. Just calling to holla at 'cha. What you got going on tonight?" he asked in his preppy voice.

"My partners and I are going to Club Magic tonight," I told him as I shut the engine off on my car and opened the door.

"I heard it's supposed to be lit tonight... something about a pajama party. My cousins and brothers are thinking about sliding down the interstate to attend."

"Y'all do that. You already know we gonna have a section to ourselves," I voiced as I hopped out of my whip, aiming for the front door of my two-bedroom, one bath, red brick home.

"Will do. How's life been treating you lately?"

"Sometimes good and sometimes bad," I laughed.

Chuckling at my remark before asking, "Dude, what in the hell you did now?"

"A bitch by the name of Jacquel saying I got her pregnant and shit. Knowing damn well that will cause some issues," I informed him as I unlocked my front door.

"Is it yours?"

"Hell fuck nawl."

"Then why she trying to pin a baby on you?"

"I guess because she wants to make sure the little bastard is well taking care of... that's the only answer I can think of."

That was the only answer I could provide because I truly believed that's what she thought. Since X and I been fucking around heavy, I didn't see a need to be dipping off in Jacquel like that. Every time I dived deep in that universal pussy, I made sure to purchase a box of rubbers and not let her put her hands on the box. So, I wasn't being a jokie ass nigga when I said that the baby wasn't mine— it wasn't.

"Them ghetto ass runts always trying to trap a nigga. Now, do you see what your mother be saying about them? I was never attracted to them loud mouthed, weave wearing, patting that dry ass shit through their funky ass bonnets, too much make-up, acrylic wearing, long, fake eyelashes, legging wearing ass hoes."

Drew had me laughing so hard that I damn near choked. It wasn't what he said, it was how he said it that had me tickled than a mug. He was imitating how ghetto broads talked.

"Mane, you finna get your ass off my line. I'm not dealing with your shit today," I told him as I began to end my laughter.

"You know I'm telling the truth," he sniggered lightly before continuing, "That fine ass chick you be around...I saw her today."

When Drew mentioned seeing X, my ears were open as I came to a complete stop in front of my refrigerator.

"Really? Where?"

"Yeah, she was in the hood up here in Auburn."

"What she was doing in the hood? What was she driving?" I questioned curiously as I headed back to the front door, Auburn bound.

"She was talking to one of the heavy hittas of Jockson's Court, and she was in a black on black Tahoe."

"Around what time you saw her?"

"About twenty minutes ago. Is her name X? If so, I been hearing her name well in the streets. She got these motherfuckers on lock."

"Aye, I'm on my way up there," I told him ready to conclude our conversation.

"A'ight, stop by my spot."

"Bet," I stated before we hung up the phone.

There was no way I was going to inform Ruger, Baked, or J-Money that X was spotted in Auburn. At the moment, I had to talk to her one on one to get us back on the right track and to see what the fuck she was doing talking to a heavy hitter. One thing I prayed for as I peeled out of my driveway, that she hadn't been on any social media sites. I wasn't ready for anything slick to come out of her mouth.

***

It took me fifty minutes to touch down in Auburn. Every time I came to the city, I fell in love with the pleasant environment. The city reminded me a lot of Des Moines, Iowa— filled with white people that always had a smiling face, shopping centers that were packed every day of the week and busy streets no matter the time of day, and tall, healthy trees and colorful plants aligned perfectly on the curb of establishments of homes and businesses.

I didn't know where to go, so I decided to cruise down South College Street in search of the black Tahoe that I knew all too well.

Not sure what I was going to say to her when I saw her, I told myself repeatedly that I wasn't going to jump down her throat for not responding to any of our texts or calls. An hour later of riding around the city, I decided to pop up in Drew's hang out spot, Jockson's Court. Soon as I turned into the heavily populated projects, I saw the black Tahoe parked behind a silver Escalade truck with platinum rims. Bypassing Drew and his brothers, I pulled my car in front of the Escalade and hopped out.

"What up, Rondon?" Drew yelled soon as he saw my face.

"What it do, mane? I'll be down there in a minute," I told him quickly as I strolled towards the Tahoe.

While posting up against the front door of the Tahoe, I dug into my front, right pocket and pulled out a cigarette and lighter. Upon me firing up the cigarette, the screen door opened, and X told a fat nigga that she would holler at him later on. Sauntering toward me, she had a blank look upon her face.

"Why haven't you been answering your phone?" I asked, blowing smoke out of my mouth.

"I was voted out, remember? There was no reason in me answering for those that thought I wasn't capable of running *my* organization, and there was certainly no need in me answering for a man that makes me feel like Tyke did and still does," she stated blankly, fumbling with the keys in her left hand.

I couldn't express the way I felt as she told me that I made her feel like her uncle did. There was no way I could beat around that bush. Hell, I barely wanted to discuss it because there was no way in hell she was going to put me in the same category as the motherfucker that possibly killed his mother to raise her.

Blowing air out of my mouth before slowly and apologetically saying, "I want to apologize for my behavior and what I said to you. You hurt my fee—" I said before she held up one finger and shook her head.

"You are good. It is what it is. My first doc' appointment is this Thursday at Doctor Duggar's office off Saint Lukes Drive. If you want, be there at nine forty-five," she breathed softly as she looked into my face with a blank facial expression.

With a huge grin on my face, I was thankful that she decided to keep the pregnancy. Reaching for her, X pulled back and shook her head.

"I want a hug. May I have one?" I asked, licking my lips.

"Nawl, I'm good Reginald. I'm sleepy, so I'm finna head up outta here. I guess I'll see you Thursday," she responded, nudging her head to the left—indicating for me to get out of her way.

Not budging, I glared at the beautiful woman that worked all of my nerves when she let anything fly out of her mouth. I was surprised at her behavior; this was the side I rarely saw of her. When she was pissed, everyone around her felt that wrath. As we played the staring game, my dick got hard, and I wanted to press it deep inside of her.

Standing in a pair of white Ugg boots, tight fitting jeans with a white belt through the loops, and a white short-sleeved Ralph Lauren shirt, X was glowing. Her once braided hair was in its natural form, flowing past her shoulders. Her natural hair was long and jet black. There was no need for her to wear weave because baby girl had mad hang time down to the middle of her back. On her face were a pair of white framed glasses, in her earlobes were small, studded diamond gold earrings, in her left nostril was a gold hoop nose ring, and in the middle of her tongue sat a gold tongue ring. No need for fake eyelashes because her real eyelashes were perfectly curled and long. The only thing that was fake on X's body were her nails, which she kept at a nice length. They weren't long, but they weren't short either.

"May I get in the truck, please?" she asked, interrupting my thoughts with her hands on her hips.

"Not until you give me a hug."

"Rondon, cut the shit out. We are just co-parenting, and we aren't on bad terms, okay? So, let things be the way they are with us."

"I'm not having that, X, and you know that."

Smacking her lips, she spat, "Go ask Jacquel for a hug. I'm very sure she would love that."

Ain't this some shit, I thought as I looked at X.

"That bitch don't mean shit to me."

"I don't either. So, with that being said... be at the doc's office... if you wanna."

"Are you hungry?"

"Nope."

"Where are you going?"

"Home."

"Which one?"

"Whichever I choose."

Exhaling sharply, I was tired of the dry, one-word conversation that we were having. All I wanted to do was make-up for my behavior. She was giving me the Tony Syndrome, and I wasn't up for it. The Tony Syndrome was when she shut down and didn't want to be bothered. Any attempt at a conversation would result in her only saying one thing and disconnecting herself from those around her.

"Will you talk to me, please?"

Growling for a while before responding, she said, "Look, what you do in your spare time is none of my business. What I do in my spare times is none of your business. We tried it. It didn't work out, so let's end this freak show. You got me pregnant. I'm keeping it. Let's move forward with that."

After she was done speaking, she roughly snatched me by the collar of my shirt and kicked me in the legs. Seeing how she was going to play with me, I laughed and let her hop in the Tahoe. As she screeched away from the curb, I ran to my whip and hopped in. After I started the engine, I zoomed behind that heifer because I was going to make things right with her. I told myself that I wasn't going to force my way on her. I wanted her to yearn for me. That would make our love making even better.

Making a left turn onto Pride Avenue, my cell phone rang. Taking it off the holster, I rejected my mother's call. She knew how to work all of my nerves, and I was still pissed at her from our prior conversation. She was not going to get the best of me today. While I jumped in the left turning lane behind X, my mother called again, and I rejected the call. Zooming through the light that intersected North Donahue Drive and Pride Avenue, my phone rang, and I was ready to curse the woman out that birthed me. I was relieved to see X's name on the screen. As I drove, I quickly fumbled with my phone to answer it.

"Hello."

"Stop following me," X commanded harshly.

"Nope."

"You made it very clear that I'm not what you want. Last week, you had time to go and fuck another bitch, but you didn't have time to follow me. So, please go ahead and follow that bitch," she spat angrily in the phone.

"You are one hard individual to be with. It's to the point I don't know what to do, X."

"You know what to do, bitch! Leave me the fuck alone. You knew what you were fucking when you decided to drop your dick off in me, Rondon. I didn't hide shit from you... oops! I couldn't because you were one of my fucking goons, nigga. You thought we were going to have a happily ever after? Nigga, you really are fucking stupid if you thought that. Now, stop fucking following me," she stated in a high-pitch tone.

I wanted to blow on that ass, but I noticed her voice went from screaming to extremely high-pitched, and I knew what that meant—she was ready to cry. Sighing heavily, I replied, "X, let's talk... please."

"Noo, I want to be left the fuck alone," she sobbed as we approached a red light, which turned green; I hated that the light changed so quickly, because I was going to get out in traffic and demand for her to talk to me.

I was about to respond until my phone beeped. Briefly taking the phone away to see who had sent me a text message, I groaned as my mother's name displayed.

"No matter where you go... I'll be on your ass," I told X, shrugging off my latest text message notification.

"Not for long," she spat as she hung up the phone.

That heifer took me on a ride for my life. I didn't know where in the hell she was going. I kept up with her until flashing lights got behind me.

Laughing hysterically before shouting, "I know this heifer did not put these motherfuckers on me."

Pulling my car over to the curb in front of a nice looking, two-story cabin like house miles away from McMillian Street, I gathered my car's information and rolled down the window. When I looked up, I saw X riding up the road with a wide smile on her face as she stuck her middle finger out of the window.

"Ouuu, you wait until this motherfucker let me go. I'mma find your ass... I'mma damn near fuck you into a coma," I announced as the white officer came close to my car.

Chapter Nineteen

Juvy

I wasn't right in the mind for several reasons. One, my adoptive family turned on me. Well, they were fake all along. Two, Flema killed herself because she must've thought that I wasn't going to be there for her or our unborn child. Three, I was forced to be an accomplice to harming someone that was ruthless toward everyone in the streets but me.

A nigga didn't know which way to turn or know what task to focus on the most. One thing I knew without a doubt, I was not going to harm X. Therefore, I had to seek out Ruger and X's help in order to aid them in killing the Jocktons and Reggio.

Reggio, his bastard sons, and I were in Alabama for four days before I decided that I had to get back to Miami. I had Flema on my mind so badly that I left the nice spot in Gulf Shores that Reggio owned. With the help from X, I fled Alabama—heading back to Miami. Once I hopped in the black Tahoe she was driving, I knew immediately that something was wrong with her. X was not her normal self; she was quiet and distant. When I finally asked her what was up, she laid it on me, and I felt her pain. She was dealing with an early pregnancy, her goons voted her out of her organization, and a past love came back from the dead—who also happened to be Reggio's son.

I was in shock at the things she told me to the point I couldn't say anything. I would've thought that Reggio wanting her dead was the issue, but it wasn't. Love was the problem; that four letter word was a motherfucker to a person that never received it except from one person—her grandmother. The same grandmother that was killed by her son, which was X's uncle, Tyke. By the time X told me that the second person she's ever loved was killed at the hands of Ruger and Rondon, she broke down and had to pull the SUV over. I never thought a broad of her caliber would know what tears were, but it was obvious that she knew.

As I thought about X while cleaning out Flema's home, I realized that X and I had much in common, especially when it came down to how we felt about the opposite sex, trust, and the ability to push people away. While I was looking at the pictures of Flema and her family, tears began to form as I thought about our younger days. She was such a loving, caring person, and I drove her mad. I was the reason she went to desperate measures, and my heart wouldn't allow me to forgive myself. I could barely say that Flema's death wasn't my fault. I was deep off in my thoughts when I felt a hand soft as cotton touch my forearm.

"How are you feeling?" Wilema's delicate voice asked as she looked at the side of my face.

"Not good, Wilema, not good," I sighed not taking my eyes off the beautiful, white and black picture of Flema, Wilema, and their stern-faced mother.

"The funeral is set for this Saturday at eleven o'clock at Friendship Missionary Baptist Church. You do know that I'm here for you if you need me, Juvy," she replied seductively as she slowly ran her hand up my right arm and across my chest.

Finding her behavior odd at a moment like this, I politely removed her hand away from me and stepped six paces away from her. *That's fucked up that Flema is getting buried on a day before Christmas Eve, and this bitch is trying to make a pass at me. Damn, she couldn't wait until her sister was in the ground,* I thought. Taking a look at the time on my watch, it read that it was 1:30 p.m. I was hoping that by me looking at my watch, it would prompt the dummy to think about something else.

"Wow. So, you are telling me that you actually had feelings for my sister?" she huffed in a jealous timbre.

With a dumbfound facial expression, I analyzed Wilema before speaking to her. Standing in a pair of olive-green pants, a black, short-sleeved shirt, and black ankle length boots, Wilema had a look on her face that didn't indicate that she was mourning. As she ran her left hand through her soft, burgundy curls, she batted her medium length, fake eyelashes while licking her thick, ruby-red lips.

"Do y'all need anything?" I inquired as I backed away from her, ignoring her question.

"Our children and me, or my family?" she stated in a matter-of-fact tone.

"Your family?"

"No, we are good," she responded, coming close to me.

Then, she continued, "Now that my sister killed herself... what's up with us raising our children?"

Completely thrown off by how Wilema was so nonchalant about Flema's actions, I shook my head without a word to say.

"Cat got your tongue, Juvy?" she laughed and then continued angrily with her hands on her thick hips, "You were so willing to be there for Flema. Why not me?"

Not wanting to hear the shit that was going to come out of her mouth, I turned on the heels of my white Air Force Ones and jetted toward the front door with Wilema on my heels asking questions.

"Why she got you all in your feelings? What was so special about her? Are you going to release my children from Tania and Fish to me?"

"Back the fuck up off me with all of those unnecessary ass questions. Mourn your damn sister instead of running behind dick that ain't stuntin' you!" I barked angrily as I turned around and faced her.

Balling up her fists, she spat nastily, "Who in the fuck do you think you are talking to like that, Juvy?"

"The only bitch in this house that's seeking attention from a nigga that's not willing to give it to her."

"Hmph," she said before continuing, "You either going to give me attention, or I will tell all of your dirty deeds to the authorities. You know I have proof of everything you've done."

Immediately, I began unclenching and clenching my jaws, ready to slam her ass into the wall. Instead, I shook my head at her and waltzed out of the door. As soon as my left foot hit the second step, she brought her ass out the door and started popping off at the mouth. My patience was growing thin and before I knew it, I snapped. Looking up at the once beautifully blue sky that turned gray within a matter of seconds of me first arriving at Flema's home, I exhaled heavily before running back on the porch and yoking that hoe up.

"If you knew what was good for you, you would shut your damn mouth. I would hate for your mother to be burying both of her daughters on the same day! Fuck you and what you thought we had. You were some easy pussy that got me all the narcotics in the world. So, fuck all that shit you talking 'bout, bitch. If you wanna go to the authorities, then be my guest and go. Best to believe you'll be dead soon as you walk out of the door! As far as the kids you gave birth to against my will, you will never get them! Judging by your behavior, I really feel that you had something to do with Flema killing herself. If I find out that you did, I swear to God I will murder you myself, bitch!"

Wilema's once jealous, angry eyes were now filled with sorrow and hurt. Her once hard demeanor disappeared, and she began to cry. As soon as her faced showed that she was sad, I pulled my hands away from her neck and walked off.

"All I wanted was for you to see me the same way you saw Flema. I wanted you to love me!" she cried as I opened the door on my Ferrari.

"Go find someone that will love your trifling ass because I'm not the nigga that's going to do it! You ain't my type! You fucked a nigga that was sleeping with your sister. Bitch, you ain't shit!" I voiced loudly as I noticed Mrs. Ross stepping out onto her porch.

Sliding my tall body into the front seat of the low sitting car, I saw Mrs. Ross and Wilema conversing. Not giving a damn about their conversation, I peeled away with my destination unknown. Halfway down the road, my cellular device started ringing. Not looking at the phone when I unlatched it from the holster or sliding my finger across the answer button, I said hello before placing the phone to my ear.

"Where in the fuck are you?" Reggio hissed.

"I'm not your fucking son, dude. You want X... you go get her your fucking self," I spat nastily before hanging up the phone.

Pissed off at Reggio thinking I was something to play with, I was ready to cut that nigga's head off. Coming to a halt at the first stop sign on Flema's street, I dialed X's number. On the third ring, she answered, "Hello."

"Mane, we gotta do something about that damn Reggio. Have you talked to Ruger? The reason I'm asking because I want to make sure that you know that Reggio is in Alabama, and he wants to have your head on a silver platter. Whatever you need me to do, I'll do it. I'm on your side."

There was a brief silence on her end, which caused me to say, "X."

"Yes," she said softly, causing my heart to warm as I pressed the gas pedal and zoomed through the four way stop sign.

"Did you hear me?"

"Yes."

"What is your response then?" I inquired curiously.

"I'll handle him. In due time, he's going to get what he's asking for," she stated in a blank tone before continuing, "I will have to call you back. Is that cool?"

"Yeah," I replied in an awkward tone before our call ended.

Not sure what to think about how blank X was about the situation at hand, I let my mind travel to back to Flema. I was in my thoughts while driving around the downtown Miami until my phone rang, and the name on the screen flashed *Tania*.

"What in the fuck do she want?" I breathed before answering the phone.

"Hello."

"Hey, Juvy. I don't know what is going on, but I'm going to flee with the kids. Fish on some more shit, and I'm completely blown by his actions with his father, Reggio," she stated in a sad tone.

"What are you talking about?" I asked, playing dumb. One thing they weren't going to do was try to set me up again. I couldn't trust anyone I've known for a long time, and the Jocktons had proven that to me.

"He's hella bent on getting his father's approval by killing you. What in the hell is going on?" she inquired as she sniffled.

"I truly have no idea. All I can say is that I don't trust you or them. All of my life, I have been lied to for that man, Reggio. I don't care what you do with the two children that you didn't birth. I don't want any parts of them."

Gasping loudly before replying, "Juvy, I didn't do anything for you not to trust me. So, please do not put me in that category with those people. Now, as far as your kids, you know I love them as my own. I will take them if need be. Are you going to still support them monetarily?"

I guess the bitch didn't hear what the fuck I said about not wanting any parts of them. Therefore, I raised my voice higher, "I... don't... want... any... dealings... with... them... kids, Tania. I'm not giving you any more money for them. Send them to their real mother... Wilema. She wants them, so she will take full responsibility!"

"Juvy, why are you being so cold to them and to me? They are a part of you just like they are her?"

"I said what I had to say. What I did was wrong. I had no business fucking around with Flema's sister in the first place. I can't look at them kids the same. Why you think I never came to a birthday party of theirs or was around them period? They are a constant reminder of the fuck up I made when I didn't make Wilema get rid of them," I spat nastily as my head began to hurt.

"You feel guilty for Flema killing herself, don't you?" Tania asked in a low tone.

Instead of me admitting that I did felt guilty, I hung up the phone. I didn't want to talk to a bitch that probably was against me for no reason. I had enough on my plate as it was, and talking about my feelings weren't up for discussion. If I was going to talk to anyone, it was going to be X, someone who didn't really know me other than the fact that I was a victim of the 2005 slaying in Kingston, Jamaica.

I was tired of riding around and thinking, so I decided to take a trip to my favorite eating establishment, Nana and Jon's Restaurant. Parking my car in the back of the diner, I sighed heavily at the same time I heard the thunder boom from the sky.

One would've never thought it was going to rain cats and dogs this morning with a sun shining so brightly with a clear sky. Soon as I stepped out of my vehicle, I felt the cold drops of rain on my head. I ran to the right side of the brown building to avoid the massive raindrops that were bound to reign down. As I approached the entrance door, I saw Flema's and Wilema's parents step out of a black, new model Porsche truck. I was truly surprised to see them together without his wife being present. As soon as she placed her eyes on me, she gave me a mean stare. I wanted to buck, but I knew it wasn't the right thing to do.

Before I opened the door of Nana and Jon's Restaurant, I softly said, "Mrs. Willington, I'm sorry for your loss."

No need in telling the fuck up of a man sorry for his loss when he didn't want to be involved with his children because of some white bitch. He didn't deserve to be spoken to in regards to Flema.

"Fuck you, Juvy. You are the reason why she killed herself in the first place," she spat in an angry tone.

"Don't do this. Let things be. Flema made that choice, not him," George spoke heavily to the sad woman.

Stunned at her reacting that way in public but not surprised one bit that she said it, I nodded my head and waltzed inside of the great smelling place. My thoughts ran wild with the possible reasons why Flema killed herself, knowing that she was pregnant with our child, until I thought about how Wilema's behavior changed.

Nawl, there isn't a way that she would've done her sister like that. She never showed signs of hating Flema. Wilema was cool being the side bitch, I thought as I took a seat at my favorite, private booth.

My booth, as I liked to call it, was located out of other customers' way. It was secluded and there was minimal traffic in the back of the diner, except for the servers. Whoever was going to serve my table would appear only twice because I made sure to tell them that I didn't want to be disturbed. Whenever I wanted some time to myself, I would come to the diner and post up. I wouldn't talk to anyone; I would sit, think, and eat. Today was definitely going to be one of those days.

"Hey, Juvy. I see you are by yourself today?" Samantha, my usual waitress, said with a smile on her face.

"Yes. Sometimes that's best, Samantha," I replied with a blank expression upon my face.

"I agree. That's why I love being to myself. It means the less trouble I will be in," she stated quickly and continued, "Are you getting the usual today?"

"No. I am going to get a large bowl of chicken and dumplings with a grilled chicken Caesar salad and lemonade to drink. Oh, yeah, add a slice of pecan pie," I voiced as I let my eyes roam over her thin, dark-skinned body.

"Sure thing. I'll be right back with your drink and dessert," she replied as she wrote my order down on a small, white notepad.

"What time do you get off?" I inquired, staring into her fake, gray pupils.

"Why, sir, so that you can take me back to your place?" she chuckled while looking into my face.

"Nope. So, you can take me to yours. I saw that nice lil' crib of yours, and I bet you look great waltzing around naked," I stated boldly as I licked my lips.

Leaning toward my ear she whispered seductively, "I get off in an hour, and I surely do look great as I stroll around *my* crib asshole naked."

"I'll be waiting right here to give you a lift to your crib," I replied back in her ear as I planted a kiss on it.

***

Since Samantha was the closest person to me, I had to step to the plate and lay it out for her. For the past two years, I saw how she stared at me whenever I strolled into the diner. I had to get some pressure off me, and the only way I knew how to do that was to fuck. I'd been doing that since Flema introduced me to sex. It was truly a stress reliever. Plus, I did my best thinking slamming my D in between a chick's legs.

Today was truly her lucky day from the time she got out of the shower until now, which was five hours later. Little ole Samantha knew how to handle my meat, and that blew my mind. I thought I was going to overpower her skinny ass from the back. Shoot, that chocolate woman touched her toes and slammed her fat monkey on my dick after she swallowed him whole. She had a nigga groaning, and I wasn't ashamed—thanks to X.

"You like that, Juvy?" she moaned aloud as her ass jiggled while I was playing with a delicate spot inside of her warm honey pot.

"Shid, hell yeah," I voiced in a sensual tone while smacking her right ass cheek.

On the sofa in the pockets of my jeans, my cell phone was ringing. Ignoring it, I continued to slam my man into her wet, steaming hot twat, and she caught that dick thrust for thrust. The mac and cheese noise was getting the best of me, causing me to pull out and tell her to come and sit on Mr. Johnson. Doing as I commanded, Samantha pushed me down onto her navy blue, two-seater sofa and straddled me. Biting down on her dark, juicy bottom lip, she slowly rubbed my condom clad man across her clit in a circular motion. When that heifer started slapping the head of my dick against her pussy, a grin spread across my face. I was happier than a fat kid not running during physical education. That broad was my type of freaky. She didn't want to be sexed; she wanted to be fucked, and I surely fucked her while she fucked me!

"Put that dick inside of you and make that pussy sing for me, Samantha," I groaned, pulling her close to me.

Ring. Ring. Ring.

Exhaling heavily because I was tired of the ringing device; my phone didn't stop us from humping the life out of each other. Once it stopped ringing, it started back again. With ole girl riding me wonderfully and me throwing my member up in her, I snatched my phone out of the front, right pants pocket and held it tightly in my hands without looking at the screen.

"Ouuu shit," I groaned as I enjoyed the slow, back and forth motion she was rendering to my guy.

Glancing at my phone, I saw that I had missed six calls from X. *Hell, I only heard my phone ring twice*, I thought as I dialed her number.

"Keep riding my dick and don't say anything," I said sternly to the black stallion, whose acne filled face was frowned because of the pleasure she was receiving.

On the fourth ring, X answered the phone in that gorgeous bossy tone of hers, "Hello."

"You rang?" I asked as I met Samantha's thrusts.

"Yeah, I wanted to know what's your intake on getting those bastards."

"We set a trap and voila, everything is solved," I tried to say in a normal voice, but I think it came out in a soft groan.

X didn't say anything for at least six seconds, and then she piped, "Juvy, are you fucking or beating your dick?"

"Fucking, yes," I replied with a smile on my face as I looked in an oval-faced Samantha.

"Oh my god, Juvy. You could've called me back when you were done. Matter of fact, do that," she chuckled loudly, and I imagined her showing her pearly whites.

Not wanting to let her off the phone, I told her that she was good, but of course, the bossy woman in her came out, "That's not right. Maybe the other person wants to moan out loud? I did, so give her that right."

At the mentioning of her moaning and enjoying our sex session, my dick got extra hard, and I told her that I would call her back soon as I was done. Hanging up the phone, I dove deep in Samantha. I wanted her ass knocked out from nutting and screaming so much. I needed her to be exhausted, so that I could curl up on the longer, navy blue sofa and talk to X until we both fell asleep on the phone.

"Yes, Juvy, right there... hit it harder... harder... harder!" Samantha yelled seductively as I lifted her bottom and punished the left side of her pussy. Her body spoke volumes as I brought it to an orgasm. That fat monkey of hers kept creaming, her body was shaking, her eyes were rolling in the back of her head, and her juicy lips were shaped like an O as she howled my name.

Moments later, she was passed out in her bed, snoring; as I was on the phone with that sexy, boss bitch, talking like we were best friends!

Chapter Twenty

Bango

It's been one helluva week without seeing Taea or my babies. Since the shooting at my wedding, they have been my number one priority. I got better because of them; they were my motivation. Even though, the twins weren't born until October 2017, I still saw them as motivation to get better and resume the man of the household status. By me imagining their precious faces kept a smile and a positive attitude about the situation I was thrown in.

"What's the move on X?" Snoogi's crackly, deep voice spat, interrupting my thoughts.

"Protect her at all costs," I voiced as I saw a tanned young chick skate out of Sonic with two stuffed brown bags and two large drinks. I wondered if that was our meal because I had the munchies like hell.

"May I ask why?" he asked quickly before the girl strolled toward the driver's side of Snoogi's white Suburban.

By the time I was getting ready to open my mouth, Snoogi's tanned hand rolled down the window and handed the chick the money for our order. He and the cute woman flirted a little, resulting in him getting her number. While his thirty-year-old ass was flirting with someone younger than him, I was in the passenger seat cracking up at the old ass lines he was using. Once he told her to have a good evening, he passed me my food and told me to answer his question. Digging through my stuffed bag for my chili cheese tater tots, I didn't answer until I popped six of them into my mouth.

"What she did wasn't for me. It was for Pops."

With a raised eyebrow, he replied, "And you believed her?"

"I talked to her face to face last week, and everything she told me, I believed. I had history with her, so I would know instantly if she was lying or not," I confessed, giving him the same eye contact that he gave me.

"I kinda figured something had happened between the two of you because you had plenty of chances to kill her."

Nodding my head, I entertained my food because I didn't need to call X and tell her that I wanted to see her. There was no telling what would happen this time. The last thing I wanted to do was implement my thoughts of lying between her legs. I really wouldn't be able to look Taea in the face afterwards.

"Have you talked to Taea today?"

"Nawl, she super pissed at me."

"Why?" Snoogi laughed while shaking his head.

"She ran into Kutta, and Kutta revealed a truth," I stated in between chewing on the rest of my tots.

"Explain."

"Taea thought that Kutta was sending her the money after my fake death. It was X sending the money."

Coming to a complete stop with opening his burger, Snoogi's thin, almost invisible lips dropped open.

"So, you are telling me that the woman that supposedly 'accidentally' shot you at your wedding sent money to your wife?" he asked dumbfounded.

"Yep," I replied, shaking my head.

"How do you know it was X who was sending the money?"

"She had a loose lip, gay nigga in her crew. I sent Bono to finesse his ass, and he started singing. That's how I knew that every Saturday, X would go to the wedding site, sit, and cry."

"Wow. Who was the loose lip nigga?"

"DB."

"I haven't seen that nigga in a while. Have you?"

"Come to think about it, I haven't. His ass is probably dead. I know his lover Silky Snake got capped down in the middle of the streets some weeks back by X's young lover, Tony."

Shaking his head, he replied, "Well, got damn."

"Snoogi, I can't have my father kill her. I need her to be protected at all costs. Do you understand me?"

He didn't respond immediately. Instead, he looked at me with a certain look in his eyes, and I knew he was about to school me on some shit.

"Do you think it's fair to Taea for you to be protecting and still lusting after a woman that has brought so much pain to y'all?"

"No, but there's more to the story."

"Are you prepared to lose Taea?"

"Yes."

Surprised at my answer, Snoogi shook his head and started the engine on the SUV. With nothing left to say, I had a strong urge to hit up X. For six hours as Snoogi and I rode around the tri-county area, I fought that urge, but I finally gave in. I pulled my cell phone out of the holster and dialed her digits. It didn't take her long to answer the phone, but when she did, I could tell that she was nervous.

"What are you doing?" I asked after her soft voice said hello.

"Lying on the sofa, trying to watch *Hidden Colors Two*."

"Where are you?" I asked at the same time Snoogi looked at me and shook his head.

"Ducked off," she laughed.

Laughing hysterically at her answer, I had to shake my head before responding, "You are one bold bitch you know that?"

"Yep."

"I'm on my way!"

"A'ight," she replied before hanging up the phone.

"Where are we going?" Snoogi asked curiously.

"*We* ain't going nowhere. I am. Take me to Grandma Toot's house," I informed him as I gave myself the pep talk that nothing was going to take place between X and me.

On the way to Grandma Toot's house, the once bright sun had disappeared and was replaced with gray clouds. I was more eager to make it to one of my hiding spots in Columbus, Georgia where X was at probably lying in the white room with nothing on but a pair of black ankle socks. Little drops of rain started pummeling the windshield, the wind started howling, and my dick started growing. The forecast was that "make a baby" type of weather.

As Snoogi left Millbrook heading back to Montgomery, he turned the radio down that was playing Oldie Goldies. He glanced at me briefly before speaking his mind. He did that shit often.

"I hope you know what you are doing. I hope you know what you are sacrificing. I really hope you know what you might be giving up for some past feelings."

Hearing every word that he said, I nodded my head and said, "Can you put the hazard lights on and drive faster?"

"Did you hear anything I just said to you?"

"Yep. Now, did you hear me when I said put on the hazard lights and drive faster?"

"Yep," he replied nonchalantly.

With a smirk on my face, I watched Snoogi zoom the SUV into the fast lane and ride that bitch out--all the way until we hit

Braisedlawn community. The closer we got to my grandmother's house, the more anxious I became. I didn't want Snoogi following me. Therefore, I had a plan to sit back and watch him peel off. Before he pulled up to Grandma Toot's front yard, I was halfway out of the truck, running toward my car until my grandmother stopped me.

"Where yo' po' ass finna go, Marcus?" she hissed at me with her hands on her hips.

"To handle some business," I told her as I noticed Snoogi was pulling off.

"Yo' ass better not be doing anything you ain't got no business doing. You know your face turns red when you are ready to have sex," she spat with a smirk on her face.

"Oh goodness, Grandma, you don't care what comes out of your mouth. You are wrong on this tip. I'll catch you later, okay?" I informed her as I strolled closer to her and placed a dry kiss on the left side of her cheek.

"Will you be in for dinner?" she probed as I began to turn around.

"Probably not."

"You better not do shit you ain't got no business doing, Marcus Johnson!"

"Okay, woman!" I yelled as I took off running toward my 2016 black on black Cadillac.

Ring. Ring. Ring.

Not paying attention to my phone until I started the engine on my whip, I peeled it away from the holster. Right when I was about to answer the thing, X had hung up. Reversing the car and dialing her number, I had to take several deep breaths. A nigga was super anxious to be in her presence. She and I had some things that had to be talked about!

"Hello," she sneezed into the phone.

"Mane, you better spray that damn Lysol while you are piling mucous all through that joint," I laughed at the same time I placed the gearshift in drive and tooted the horn at my grandmother.

"Will you stop and get something to eat? I'll pay you when you get here?" she asked in that same young, innocent voice that I grew to love when we were younger.

"Nope," I chuckled.

"Why?" she pouted.

"I plan on cooking your favorite meal. We have some shit to talk about, X, and I won't let it rest until it's all out on the table."

"What do you want to talk about?"

"I'm not going to tell you. I want to see your facial expression. You know? Just like I know that you went through basic training and all of that military shit... I have to see your eyes when we talk."

"Understandable... is it about why I am the way I am or the way I'm perceived?"

"All that... I'll be there in about an hour."

"Okay," she replied nervously.

Right then, I knew I had to nip that shit in the bud. "I don't want that Queenpin X present. I need X'Zeryka present... the one I fell in love with. That's the person I need up front and center, okay?"

"Fell in love with? Um, you know what? Don't explain that. But umm... okay...yeah...Bango, I feel uncomfortable being X'Zeryka. Can we skip that talk?" she responded in that same nervous tone.

"Nope. I need to know it all from the beginning to the end. I need to know... my marriage depends on your answers, X. You have to give me closure, and I have to give you closure as well."

"Okay."

"I'll be there before you know it."

"Okay."

Not wanting to end the call, I had to. The entire drive out of Montgomery, Alabama to Columbus, Georgia, I had thousands of questions in my head. It was time for me to know the entire truth about her and the feelings she possessed for me. There was so much shit that we did to each other it wasn't real. I endured the worst, but I knew there was a reason for it all. There could've been a fuck up on the deliverer's end. One way or another, X'Zeryka

Nicole Toole was going to tell me everything that I wanted to know.

***

It was 5:45 p.m, when I touched down at my Colonial style home in Columbus, Georgia. I drove my car into the garage that was located in the back of the house. Upon me getting out of the car, running toward the back porch, X was standing at the door in a pair of white jogging pants, white sports bra, and the goofiest pair of Donald Duck house shoes. Not able to catch my balance from running rapidly and hopping onto the fourth step, I slid into X, knocking her down. Laughter seeped out of our mouths as we lay on the ground. Getting up slowly ensuring not to fall again, I held out my hand for her to take it. It took her a while to do so, but when she did, her eyes fell to the dark brown floor of the hangout area.

"Well, should we begin the talking now?" she asked before biting down on her bottom lip, still not giving me any eye contact.

"Yeah," I replied in a low tone as I pulled her close to me and ran my tongue against her lips before sticking my tongue in her mouth.

Trying to pull away, I wouldn't let her. Finessing my tongue in and out of her mouth while keeping my hands from picking her up, my dick pressed against her spot, which caused her to groan and reciprocate the kiss. For a while, we stood there in the backdoor kissing each other as if we didn't have a care in the world.

Ring. Ring. Ring.

Her phone was going off in the white room, and that little fucker was the reason she pulled away from me. I was two-sided about the situation because I missed X'Zeryka's kisses and her womanly touch. Yet, I knew I was in the wrong. Running toward the ringing phone, X's ass was wobbling all over the place and my eyes didn't leave her backside.

Jesus, help me. I went before you and made a vow to love Taea. Take this temptation away, please, I prayed as I slowly walked behind X with a severe hard on.

"I will have to call you back. Is that cool?" she voiced lightly in the phone.

The person on the other end must've said yes because she hung the phone up and threw it on the sofa. Sighing heavily, she spoke loud and clear, "You wanted to talk, and that is all that we are going to do."

"I'm cool with that," I said, completely unsure if I was truly okay with it.

"What do you want to know?" she asked as she took a seat on the long, white sofa.

"How long did you cry when you thought I was dead?" I questioned as I kicked off my shoes and placed them against the wall, closest to the white room.

"I stopped crying over you when I heard your voice some weeks back."

"Did you really shut the streets down because of how you were feeling about the situation of me being 'dead'?"

"Yes."

"Why did you send the money to Taea?"

"Apology money."

"How long was you going to send it?"

"For eighteen years."

That comment blew my damn mind. She was basically going to take care of my twins until they reached a legal age. That thought alone made me feel some type of way about her, and it wasn't a bad feeling that I possessed. Quickly strolling toward X, I couldn't control my thoughts of pinning her down on the sofa, or it could be that I didn't want to control them. Scooping her up against her will, I laid her on her back and I connected my face with hers, entangling our tongues, in a deep, passionate kiss. She tried to fight me off, but I pinned her hands above her head as I pressed my hard dick in between her legs.

"No, Bango, we can't do this. We need to talk, and I have to get these things off my chest before it cripples me. You need to know everything so that we can have a clean slate and move forward with our lives without each other."

"Ugggh," I groaned in disappointment at how right she was, but I didn't move until I slipped my fingers into her panties and tickled that monkey.

That pussy got so wet that my mouth started to salivate. As she cooed my name, I stripped her jogging pants off in a flash.

"No, Bango, one of us gotta be sane, and I'm choosing to be that person. Stop, so that we can talk," she said in a not so convincing timbre.

"All I want to do is see you nut, and I promise you can put your pants back on," I told her as I bit down hard on the right corner of my bottom lip as I threw her jogging pants on the ground.

"Nooo," she groaned soon as I started licking on her belly button and toying with that cat of hers.

"I can't help it, X'Zeryka. Just this one time, give me what I want," I begged as I blew on her cat.

"It's not right. I'm a lot of things, but I don't fuck with married men," she cried.

Her comment was supposed to have triggered for me to stop, but it didn't. It fueled me to work my fingers faster while sticking my mouth on her bud. The instant shaking of her legs, the howls that escaped her mouth, and the sweet taste of honey killed the image of seeing the gold wedding band on my left ring finger. Going before God, Taea, and our families were a distant memory as I unbuttoned and pulled down my pants while tasting the best pussy I ever had.

Her juices were leaking out of her like running water out of a faucet; I was used to her being super wet but not this wet. I guessed it had a lot to do with her being pregnant for that fuck nigga, Rondon. Growing angry with her for letting him knock her up, I rushed my dick inside of her.

"Oh God, Bango, don.. don't... we can stop at any moment, okay?" she said in a scared tone as she looked at me with those brown eyes.

"Shut the fuck up, X'Zeryka. Whatever happens happens, man. You won't have to answer to my infidelity, I will. Now enjoy the dick," I voiced sternly as I passionately rotated my man inside of her.

"I can't. I feel wrong having sex with you while being pregnant with another man's child," she voiced in an awkward tone at the same time her pussy muscles clenched tightly around my D.

With an angry facial expression and a hard dick, I showed her just what the fuck I meant about shutting up. I let her know that I was punishing and pleasing her at the same time. I let her know that I was upset at all the choices she made after she turned sixteen until now. At the same time, I always showed that I still loved her.

Her once rigid body relaxed, and she started throwing that monkey on me. The thunder sounded off at the same time X'Zeryka moaned my name and exploded all over my abdomen region and white sofa.

"Yo' ass gonna help me clean this up," I laughed as I started to slow stroke that snatch.

"Un huhhh," she groaned before telling me that she wanted to get on top.

When that heifer placed that fat, bald pussy on my light-skinned, fat, eight inches of dick, I hollered, "Good fucking lawd!"

She was the captain of my boat, and I was sitting back with my hands behind my head, enjoying everything that she threw my way. Our eyes were locked into each other, and I could tell that I wasn't the only one wishing that we could turn the hands of time. The once fast motion she rendered to me was dumbed down a lot, and she started making love to the kid. The way she showed love to both of our bodies brought tears streaming down our faces, and that caused the most heartfelt kiss and orgasm to escape both of our mouths. With our bodies still connected to each other after that wonderful pleasure, there was nothing that I could think about—not my wife, kids, current situation with my father, not the past, and certainly not her punk ass baby daddy.

Eyes low to the ground, X stated, "I'll take a shower upstairs."

"You got your nut, and now your ass is running off," I replied. I was kind of hurt.

"That's not true," she replied, still not looking at me.

"Got damn it, X'Zeryka! Look at me!"

When she lifted her head, I hated that I told her to look at me because her eyes were so teary that I knew her vision was blurry. One blink and the floodgates opened followed by her crying that she was sorry for everything that happened to me and Taea, she was even sorry that she was born, and hoped that Reggio ended her life.

Now that was fucking mind blowing, and I didn't even know what to say. I knew what to do... that was be her friend— something that she hadn't known since we were younger.

"I'm never going anywhere, X'Zeryka. I should've never let you get too big for the breeches that you already had on. At this point, I think I'm willing to risk losing my wife for you," I voiced as I held her tightly all the while placing kisses on her forehead.

....

About the Author

TN Jones was born and raised Alabama. She currently resides in her native state with her daughter. Growing up, TN Jones always had a passion for reading and writing. She began writing short stories when she was a young teen. As a college student, TN Jones enjoyed writing academic research papers, which heightened her passion for writing.

In 2015, TN Jones started working on her first book, *Disloyal: Revenge of a Broken Heart*. TN Jones will write in the following genres: Contemporary Fiction, Urban Fiction, Mystery/Suspense, Interracial/Urban Romance, Dark Erotica, Paranormal, and Fantasy Fiction.

Published novels by TN Jones: *Disloyal: Revenge of a Broken Heart*, *Disloyal 2: A Woman's Revenge*, *Disloyal 3: A Woman's Revenge*, *A Sucka in Love for a Thug*, *If You'll Give Me Your Heart 1-2*, *By Any Means: Going Against the Grain 1-2*, *The Sins of Love: Finessing the Enemies 1-2*, and *Caught Up In a D-Boy's Illest Love 1-2*.

Upcoming novels by TN Jones: *Choosing To Love a Lady Thug 4*, *The Sins of Love: Finessing the Enemies 3*, and *Caught Up In a D-Boy's Illest Love 3*.

Thank you for reading *Choosing To Love a Lady Thug 3*. Please leave an honest review under the book title on Amazon's page.

For future book details, please visit any of the following links:

Amazon Author page: https://www.amazon.com/tnjones666

Facebook: https://www.facebook.com/novelisttnjones/

Goodreads: https://www.goodreads.com/author/show/14918893.TN_Jones:

Google+: https://www.plus.google.com/u/1/communities/115057649956960 897339

Instagram: https://www.instagram.com/tnjones666

Twitter: https://twitter.com/TNHarris6.

You are welcome to email her: tnjones666@gmail.com; as well as chat with her daily in the Facebook group, **It's Just Me...TN Jones**.